THE SECRET OF THE SILVER STAR

Outlaw Vince Lange hides a deadly secret: he is really Deputy Marshal Charlie Dane, working undercover to bring down the Carlin gang. When a heavy snowstorm traps the bandits in their hideout, life becomes more difficult for Dane when Frank Carlin sends him and another outlaw to fetch supplies — but only Dane returns, leaving three bodies and a burned-out ranch behind. Deciding to split the gang and head for the nearest town, Carlin gives Dane a terrible task to complete . . .

AMOS CARR

THE SECRET OF THE SILVER STAR

Complete and Unabridged

LINFORD
Leicester

First published in Great Britain in 2015 by
Robert Hale Limited
London

First Linford Edition
published 2017
by arrangement with
Robert Hale
an imprint of The Crowood Press
Wiltshire

A catalogue record for this book is available
from the British Library.

ISBN 978–1–4448–3270–9

Published by
F. A. Thorpe (Publishing)
Anstey, Leicestershire

Set by Words & Graphics Ltd.
Anstey, Leicestershire
Printed and bound in Great Britain by
T. J. International Ltd., Padstow, Cornwall

This book is printed on acid-free paper

1

The Carlin gang was galloping frantically, flat out, hell for leather, as though Satan himself was hot on their tail ends and burning their backsides with his foul, black breath. They were travelling across the wide, flat brush land towards the foothills of the saw-toothed mountains, with tops that were always touched with white, even in the height of summer.

The riders had fanned out wide, each one desperately forging his own ragged path in between the scattered boulders and patches of sagebrush. The horse's hoofs kicked up spumes of grit and stones along with clouds of dirt and dust as they hurtled along.

'C'mon, you sorry lot, get a damn move on! We ain't got much time!' Carlin yelled back over his shoulder, the words scattering behind him on the wind.

'I see it, boss! One good push and

we're home free!'

The call came from the lead man as they spurred their tiring animals on even harder. 'C'mon, Benson! Fall behind and you bloody well get left there!'

Carlin had spotted a lone rider lagging way behind the rest. At that shout, the man jammed his sharply rowelled spurs even harder into the scrawny animal's already bleeding sides, somehow managing to force just another ounce of speed from the desperately weary creature.

Well-known to kill his own men if they looked as though they weren't pulling their weight, Frank Carlin didn't suffer fools gladly. If a man fell too far behind, chances were damn strong that he'd get caught, even if the rest managed to escape. Once in custody, any one of them would be singing like a canary, and the rest of the gang would be in danger of capture. There is definitely no honour among thieves. Carlin couldn't risk that happening.

They were pushing their mounts to the limit and way beyond, and they knew it.

Foam was flying from the animals wet, lathered shoulders, the blood on their sides mixed with the sweat and sprayed out in pink, frothing globules as they were spurred even more urgently onward.

As well as their spurs, the men were using their reins as switches, leaning forward, swinging the leathers from side to side, lashing hard across their mount's necks, then whacking at their pumping quarters, trying desperately to make them move even faster, to give just that ounce more push.

And well they might. It wasn't the Devil as such who was on their fast fleeing tails, but the Viper Creek posse. The lawmen were just about a day behind and the Carlin gang needed to get up past those dark, rough foothills real fast.

They had to get way up high into the rocky mountainous area where their long-term hideout was situated, and the tracking of them would be nigh on impossible.

Right now, though, down in the scrubby, sandy brush lands, they were way too easily followed. Hell, even a blind man on a blind mule could follow their line across that ground. Once in amongst the mountains, though, it would take a top class expert to spot the tracks. Even an Indian would be hard pushed to see them up there.

The fleeing men could just about see their target as they approached, but only because they all knew very well where it was, and were actively looking out for it. When they reached the long, arrow shaped finger of jagged rocks projecting from the foot of the mountain, only then would they be almost sure of safety.

The only man who wasn't looking forward to the stay in the hideout this time was Vince Lange. He'd lived with the Carlin gang for nigh on two years and stayed in the cave a fair few times. This time, though, he was fervently hoping it would be his last stay. He was getting closer to his goal now, he could feel it.

He was also getting more than just a little tired of the constant pretence he was having to live under. The pressure was beginning to have an effect on his nerves.

'Move your sorry backsides, fellers, we're nigh on home!'

Carlin urged them on again, his harsh voice carrying back to them on the bitter air.

As they rounded the outcrop, the ground was scattered with boulders, rockslides and rough scree. All of which had been broken away from the face of the mountains over the centuries, by the wicked winds and vicious flash floods which permanently tormented the area.

No one would ever be able to follow their tracks over such rough ground, the mountains were deeply cut and scarred by the weather. Jagged, yawning fissures, deep cracks and holes covered the steep frontage of the long line of blue monoliths. Boulders the size of small houses were dotted across the flat land at their feet.

The gang careened around the finger of rock at the foot of the mountain and hit the rougher ground; as they turned the corner, their headlong flight skidded to a halt, kicking up the stones and scree around them. The weary group gathered in a bunch at the rent in the rock.

They weren't safe yet, though.

Once standing still at last, the panting horses snorted and shook their heads, splashes of thick, blood-soaked foam dripped from their sweat-lathered necks. Their flanks and sides were heaving, their nostrils stretched wide as they gasped the cold air deep into their raw lungs. One of them gave a rasping cough.

The air had become bitterly cold very quickly, carrying along with it the sharp and biting smell of snow. The deeply glowering, almost black clouds sitting heavily on the white heads of the mountains, held the solemn promise of a powerful snowstorm soon to come.

The wind was almost non-existent down where the men were gathered, so close in to the shelter of the mountains, but they could hear it howling loudly and whistling fiercely around the fissures and boulders high above them.

Two paths led upwards from the place where the Carlin gang had stopped. The most obvious of them climbed straight up the outside of the mountain, up to Heaven knows where. None of them had ever even bothered to take that perilous track. The other way was narrower, but not as steep and headed off behind a large rock fall in the opposite direction.

This narrow path to the cave was dimly-lit at the best of times, surrounded as it was by huge rocky overhangs. This time, though, as the temperature was dropping moment by moment, and the first small flakes of snow began to tumble slowly from the ever-darkening sky, the way became darker and even more difficult.

The men needed to be able to see the trail ahead, but couldn't risk setting light to their torches just yet, the glow might still be seen from the flat land, although the snow would surely soon send any posse running for home.

This first snowfall of the year was lightweight as yet, though, not the full-blown blinding whiteout which would be certain to follow in a very short time. The need to get up into the cave system as soon as possible was even keener now. It looked very much as if their stay in their hideout this time was going to be a hell of a long one.

At the almost inevitable thought of that scenario, Lange sighed deeply.

Carlin barked out his orders.

'Mendoza, take the lead. Pronto. Lange, you bring up the rear. And keep your damned eyes skinned!'

The members of the gang had swapped and changed over the years; mostly they'd been killed in fights or shoot-outs, but there was always Frank Carlin.

Thick, bushy white hair curled over his dirty collar and around his shoulders, his skin was as tanned and cracked as beat up old leather. He sported an untidy, drooping moustache, yellowing and patchily browned by the thin roll-ups which hung almost constantly from his equally thin lips. The silver-grey stubble on his face was almost thick enough to strike a Lucifer on. Carlin's cold, pale blue eyes, constantly moving, always on the lookout, struck raw fear deep into the hearts of anyone who might have ever thought about crossing him. Mostly, though, if they crossed him, they died.

Frank Carlin was a damned hard man to ride with, but he was an even harder one to leave. He had a quick and real evil temper, thinking nothing of dispensing swift, hard justice from the muzzle of his Colt or the cold steel of his hunting knife.

He had no room for slackers or time wasters. Once in his gang, you were in there for keeps. He couldn't risk some stray dog coming and going, and maybe telling anyone else about the hideout.

Carlin was well-known and much wanted in a great many places, some of the five men riding with him were almost as wanted. Their faces graced the office walls of many a lawman right across the country.

The gang was just about running out of banks, stores and telegraph offices to hit now. Carlin's leathery face had become way too recognizable in most of the towns close by, and now they had to ride further afield to pick up their ill-gotten gains, the time they had for safely getting back to their hideout was narrowing fast.

The only way for the gang to find more targets would be to abandon their comfortable cave and find themselves a new hideout some place. They were all reluctant to do that, though. They doubted there was any other place that would suit them as well as this did.

The cave had gradually become their home, for some of them it was probably the only permanent home they'd ever really known.

This time, Carlin and his men had just about scraped their sorry backsides out of the town of Viper Creek, before the posse was sworn in and mounted up. The sheriff's men were close on the gang's heels now.

Less than a day separated the two groups, but once Carlin's gang reached the mountains, they knew they'd be able to relax. Then they could watch the posse swing on past their hideout and carry on riding a long, straight trail to nowhere, with no one at the end of it.

Or — until they returned to the town of Viper Creek, empty-handed.

*   *   *

The snow, in one way at least, was damn good news for the gang, as it meant the posse would have to turn back soon, or risk being caught out in the blizzard. Snow was real dangerous stuff, especially in such quantity. The posse would have to be plain stupid to carry on riding through it, not knowing for sure where the trail would lead them.

Once the snow was lying thick on the ground, it would more than cover any tracks the gang may have left. There was no chance then, not a chance in hell, of the sheriff and his men ever finding them holed away up there.

When all the men had finally reached the fissure, they dismounted, easing themselves automatically into single

11

file. Mendoza led the way up the trail, followed closely by Carlin, with the rest strung out behind. Lange was reluctantly riding drag, constantly checking for any sight of the following posse through the rapidly darkening evening.

Struggling slowly up the treacherous track in single file, the train of tired men and bone weary horses squeezed themselves around a tall, jagged slice of ruggedly weathered rock. Behind that, yet another sharp bend they'd nicknamed the Devil's Elbow led them on to the right path for the tunnel.

'C'mon, you sorry lot! Get a move on!' Carlin yelled over the noise of the wind.

They took the tunnel climb carefully, all the while pushing on just as fast as they dared up the steep path. The men were eager to reach the warmth and safety of the cave as soon as possible; the cold was catching up with them fast now.

Had they used the other ragged path which wound its treacherous way up the outside of the craggy rock face, heading on upwards to who knew where, they'd have been too easily spotted from the flat lands below. Even with each man leading their sweating, panting mounts upward in single file, a slowly moving, heavily laden train of horses and men scaling an apparently sheer cliff face, would be pretty darned hard to miss.

The entrance to the hideout could be easily missed by anyone who didn't know of its existence, surrounded as it was by scrubby brush and piles of large fallen boulders. Anyone who was unaware of it would just see it as another dark, ragged scar among all the others dotted about on the craggy mountain face.

Way back, someone who must have been one hell of a desperate guy, had managed to find his way up that short, narrow track, from the rugged flatlands and into one of the fissures. From there he had carried on up the sloping, narrow dogleg of a tunnel, and into a large cave.

Over the years following that discovery, stories about the place were bandied around, until they reached the ears of Frank Carlin. Since then, he and his men had turned the place into the perfect hideout. They'd spent time stocking it up with stores of dry goods, barrels of water and any other things they might need for a prolonged stay.

Niches had been hacked out of the walls of the cave to store things in and right up high, one of them had been filled with a stock of ammunition, well out of the reach of any wandering animal that might just manage to find its way in.

The living area of the cave was tucked right away at the back of the sloping, serpentine tunnel, way beyond the main fissure. It was all but invisible, even to those few who actually knew it was there. The entrance was low but it was wide, the horses could just about pass through with their saddle-bags on, but not with riders atop.

Heaps of boulders surrounded the cave mouth, making it even more inconspicuous. A crudely made 'gate' of brushwood and rough timbers was wedged into the gap. These precautions all helped keep the cave and its precious contents safe from predators.

Although there wasn't much chance of any wild animal happening upon it, the gang closed the cave up tightly behind them when they left, then each of the men would relieve himself somewhere close to the entrance.

Wild animals usually avoided areas where the man scent was strong. That meant there would be very little risk of the gang turning up to the hideout to find an angry bear, or mountain lion in residence.

'We there fellers, ees OK now!'

A shout from the Mex up ahead told the rear men he'd reached the cave entrance at last. He and Carlin began to open up the hideout while the others waited behind them. The snow was just beginning to get heavier and the cold was becoming more intense.

The wind had changed direction by then and was starting to swirl the fat flakes around the men and their mounts. Their breath was beginning to hang in frozen clouds as the men pulled their collars up high against the biting wind. Some were no doubt wishing they'd worn their heavy sheepskin jackets.

The good thing about this sudden heavy snow was that the posse would definitely have given up and gone back home by now. No one would want to risk being caught out in a blizzard as intense as this one was going to be, judging by the weight of the ominous black clouds now rolling and tumbling overhead.

The entrance was quickly unblocked, brush and boulders cleared away, and the men and their weary, panting mounts edged into the marginally warmer tunnel in single file. The roof gradually became higher and from there, the fissure opened into a substantial D shaped cave.

Mendoza, followed by the rest of the gang, entered slowly. Torches were lit and the men proceeded up and into the main cave.

The cave itself was plenty tall enough for just about anyone to stand up in comfortably and more than wide enough for a fairly large group of men, along with

16

their mounts, to hole up in until danger was past.

'Home sweet home, eh, fellers?' Carlin remarked, to no one in particular.

The narrow entrance could also be closed from the inside, by another roughly woven brushwood 'door', left standing just inside the entrance. The last man in would push it up hard against the opening. This served to further disguise their hideout from prying eyes and prevented most of the wind from entering, thus keeping the place a tad warmer than it could have been otherwise.

'All in, boss!' Lange called out.

Bringing up the rear, Lange pushed his horse in behind the rest and heaved the makeshift door back across the opening, then reluctantly followed the rest of the men along the tunnel. He really wasn't happy about spending another winter stuck up in the cave with the Carlin gang.

It had to be done, though, so he would do it, yet again, but that sure didn't mean he liked it. It was getting harder each time. He could only hope this would be the last damn time he'd need to do it, then he could go and get on with the rest of his life.

The sides of the dark passage had been worn to a smooth shine in places, where saddles and packs had rubbed against the walls over the years. Those hombres who stood anything above average height had the need to duck their heads when they entered the tunnel, in order to avoid a skull battering from the jagged rock roof.

The weary horses were quickly corralled behind a stout rope at the rounded side of the cave. The men placed the torches into their rocky holders, lit the lanterns and tossed their bedrolls, saddle-bags and other kit around the outer edges of the cave.

The cave floor was mostly sandy, scattered about with areas of bedrock and boulders, which were way too large to move, so the men bedded themselves down in the softer areas.

Beyond this wide, habitable cave was another tunnel, shorter, lower and more winding, which led out to another face of the rugged, steep-sided mountains. That entrance could also be blockaded with a makeshift door, similar to the main one.

Beyond that opening in turn, was an even denser and much steeper, sparsely forested region. That whole area was covered by huge and deadly rock formations and small raggedy stands of dark and scrawny Ponderosa pine. It was an area so ferociously wild, it would be mighty difficult for anyone, even the Indians, to traverse it.

Perched just outside of that other entrance was a natural ledge, big enough to build a fair cooking fire on. Carlin's gang was nothing if not organized. Which was how they'd managed to escape capture for so many years. No one had been able to find them tucked away up there.

This fortress could be defended easily against all-comers, by this rag-tag handful of men, just as long as they had enough ammunition to hold off their attackers, and they did have plenty.

The stores of food meant they would be able to hold off any attack for many days, even weeks. Although, given the inaccessibility of the place, it was doubtful that anyone would ever find them once they'd holed up.

There was plenty of rotgut stashed away in the cave too, they'd made damn sure of that, and always after a good heist, they celebrated hard, until they passed out wherever they dropped. Mostly the banter was good-natured, but sometimes arguments broke out, then Carlin had to step in and straighten them out. He bragged he'd never yet lost a man in the cave.

There was just one real rule in there, no weapons. A stray bullet could bring the roof down on them. Carlin confiscated all their weapons, both guns and knives, just as soon as they were in the hideout, storing them in a strongbox, over which he draped a thick blanket. He used that same box as his seat and slept right beside it. He was the only one who kept a gun about his person in the cave.

The men were allowed to take guns out to hunt for game whilst they were holed up in there, fresh meat was always needed, but their irons had to be handed in just as soon as the men got back. There was no sense putting any sort of temptation within their reach.

Carlin barked out his orders as he confiscated their weapons and the men settled themselves in.

'Morten, chuck duty. Lange, help him out. Skinner and Mendoza, sort the horses. Benson, stash the stuff. And hurry up, all of you, I'm gettin' damn hungry.'

He took a long chain with a key on it from around his neck and threw it over to Benson, who caught it deftly and headed to the furthest corner of the cave with it. There, beneath a small natural overhang, was a deeply dug hollow close in beside the rock wall.

A large boulder disguised the hollow and with some effort, Benson moved the boulder aside enough to expose the hiding place. From within it, after much grunting and puffing, he heaved out a large strongbox.

Benson crossed over to the horses, Mendoza and Skinner passed him the money and other valuables from their saddle-bags, Benson piled them up beside the strongbox. He opened the box and almost reverentially, took a long, hard, mouth-watering look at its contents.

There were stacks of bank notes and bags of coins of all denominations. A smaller box inside the large one, held jewellery, watches and other small personal belongings the gang had taken from people they'd robbed.

Benson quickly piled their latest ill-gotten gains in the box and with a final, covetous stroke of the proceeds, slammed the lid shut, locking it tight and forcing it with some difficulty back into its deep hiding place.

He rolled the boulder into place over the top of the box then threw the key back to Carlin, who caught it easily and hung it back round his neck, tucking it down deep into his shirt.

Carlin divided some of the stash fairly between them whenever they left to go into a town. They had money for drinks, cards and women; he needed to keep his men happy and plenty of money would help do just that.

One-eyed Jack went out to the back entrance of the cave and soon got a fire going on the small flat area, using the piles of brushwood and dried buffalo chips they kept in the tunnels.

Lange busied himself getting out the provisions they needed for the evening meal. Soon there was a billy on the boil, with a black pot full of red beans and bacon hanging on the frame above the flames.

While Benson was stashing the takings, Mendoza and Skinner had been sorting out the horses, taking off their gear and fastening them in securely behind the rope. They fed and watered the heavily sweating creatures, then began roughly grooming them, switching the sweat and blood from their hides with twigs and scraping them down with hands full of straw.

The tired animals shuffled as they

tried to ease their aching bones, twitching their ears and snorting softly in the shadows, resting weary heads on warm soft rumps, chewing gently, and swishing their tails contentedly at last. Clouds of steam drifted up from their wet backs as they slowly dried out. Whichever horse it was that had been coughing in the cold outside the cave, was quiet now.

The hideout was quickly warming up with the combined heat from animals and men. It was becoming much more comfortable, chaps, jackets and hats had been discarded, shirtsleeves pushed up above the elbows.

Carlin spread his blanket out on the floor beside the box of weapons, rolled and lit a thin cigarette then laid down, using his saddle-bags as a pillow. With his hands locked behind his head, he sighed with contentment. All he needed now was a strong cup of Arbuckle's, a plate of hot tucker and he'd be in heaven.

He knew he had a good group of men around him right now, he could trust them to watch one another's backs and more importantly, to watch his back. He knew they'd be stuck up here for a good few weeks, maybe more this time. For the most part, they all got along well, which was a damn good job. It was a small space for six boisterous men to be stuck in for so long.

Vince Lange, though, reckoned it was far too small a space to be stuck in with these particular men for any length of time at all, but he had to be there. He'd been given no real choice in the matter.

He'd just have to shrug his shoulders and get on with it, again.

2

Three weeks into their latest stay in the cave, the Carlin gang had made it comfortable once more. It was warm, there was good food and plenty of coffee, smokes, cards, booze and banter; what more could they have asked for?

They were well-organized; taking it in turns to hunt, cook, keep the fire stoked up, feed and clean out the horses and any other daily tasks that might need doing. Someone was nearly always on watch and the fire outside the rear entrance burned low, day and night.

A large pot of strong coffee was perched permanently on a flat rock to the side of the fire, where the embers kept it hot. It needed only a couple of minutes on the flames to come back to the boil again when any of them wanted a brew.

One or two of the men went out from the cave every so often, ploughing their way through the drifts and down to the flat lands, both to give the horses some much needed exercise and to hunt for fresh food. There were still a few mountain hares about and every once in a while a stray deer or mountain goat would wander close by and be picked off.

There was no chance now of the men's tracks being discovered. The posse wouldn't be straying far away from their homes in that weather. All in all, life was going pretty good for the Carlin gang right about then.

The numbers of Carlin's followers had changed often over the years. Six men were running in the gang now. Carlin's right-hand man was Manuel Mendoza, a stocky, greasy-looking Mexican, sporting many scars and wearing a battered and dirty sombrero.

Mendoza did carry a gun, but preferred using his knives. One of the most evil and perverted men in the gang, his knives were mostly used for his own twisted sense of 'fun'. He liked nothing more than to cut the women he bedded, and he laughingly boasted to anyone who would listen, about just how many women carried his marks.

Sam Skinner, a tall gangling streak of misery, looked like an undertaker with a bowed stance and skeletal countenance. Skinner was so tall he had gotten into the habit of stooping when talking to folk; this had turned into a permanent stoop, as if his spine had fused itself into position, so that now he even walked about bent forward.

One-eyed Jack Morten had been named, not very imaginatively, for an old injury. A gunfight had taken his eye, leaving an ugly scar in its place and he sported a black eye patch. He favoured all black clothes, including a stovepipe hat, the brim of which he'd pierced holes in, fastening a rawhide thong through to hold it on his head.

Harry Benson wore a short, pointed beard and badly broken nose, which sat crookedly on his scarred face. One scar, running deep and wide down his cheek, was so thick that no hair grew over it.

Two fingers missing from his left hand were the result of a stray bullet. He'd learned to shoot again, with a fair amount of accuracy after he lost his fingers.

Only problem was, Benson was way too quick to use bullets rather than words to solve any arguments. He was the main reason Carlin took care of the guns; Benson would kill the whole damn lot of them if he went stir crazy in the cave. Or if he thought he was being cheated at cards, or even if he thought one of the others looked wrongly at him; he used his guns the way most men used their fists.

The latest and youngest recruit to the Carlin gang was Vince Lange, an all-out slacker and no-good bum, a man who'd do pretty much anything for a quick buck. He'd been running with the gang for almost two years now. A quiet man, Lange mostly held himself aside from the rest. He was a reader and often had a book or broadsheet of some sort in his pack, much to the amusement of the others. Vince Lange was just the sort of guy the boss liked to have around him.

Carlin had picked him up in Fresno, where Lange had been drifting looking for work. The older man had taken to him straight away; there was something about the kid that he kind of liked. Over a drink at some cheap flophouse, Carlin suggested that Lange join his gang, told him he'd never have to go looking for work again if he did. Lange was intelligent, literate and well-built.

His physique, along with a pair of piercing brown eyes and thick wavy hair hanging loosely over his collar, made him very popular with the ladies. Frank Carlin had seen that and he knew that, for the ladies, Lange needed money. It had sounded like a good proposition for them both at the time.

However, Vince Lange was carrying a secret around with him. It was something he could never afford for Carlin and his gang to discover. Lange's way of protecting that secret was to stick to himself and spend his spare time reading, not joining in with the general conversations. When they all celebrated with the rotgut whiskey they had stashed in the cave, he was careful only to drink in moderation. He knew that if any one of them, by any means at all, should uncover his secret, he would most definitely be a dead man. And he also knew he would die in the most horrible of ways at the hands of the rest of the gang. Of that there was absolutely no doubt.

The others didn't suspect anything, just reckoned he was odd, reading all the time. None of them had any truck with book learning, mostly they had just about enough reading to get by from day to day and guessed that was about as much as they'd ever be needing.

Carlin could read a tad more, at least enough to be able to read pretty much everything that Lange read. He sometimes borrowed a book or pamphlet from the kid, even though he didn't understand many of the longer words.

Mendoza couldn't read at all, reckoning he knew well enough where the whorehouses and bars were just by looking, he didn't need to be able to read where they were. They were outlaws, not schoolmarms, he argued, so what the hell was the point of book learning?

Oft times the others called Lange 'the Preacher', because of his reading. He took their taunts in good part, poking equal fun back at them for not being able to read properly. It was all just good-natured banter. Or as good-natured as it could be, considering he had to keep his wits so sharp all the time he was with them.

During their stays in the cave since he'd hooked up with Carlin, Lange had made himself a comfortable space in one corner, where he'd stashed a small selection of reading matter. With lanterns flickering and book in hand, he was mostly content.

The noise from the rest of the gang washed over him for the most part, unless someone mentioned his name and then he took notice. He never stirred to let them know he'd heard anything, just tuned his sharp ears in to the conversation, listening for any other mention of him, trying to figure out why they were talking about him.

He had to be on his guard all the time. He had to protect his secret at all costs.

His life depended on it.

After three long weeks and with the snow outside the cave now standing four feet deep and more in the still un-trodden areas, it was certain sure that nobody in their right minds would be heading their way any time soon. The gang knew they would be safe around the place for the rest of the winter.

It was warmer and getting stuffier and smellier in the cave now. The horses' muck was thrown out of the rear opening and down the mountainside into the small valley. Despite that, there was still enough of their waste left to create an acrid, sharp ammonia stench in the cave.

That, mingled with cigarette smoke, whiskey fumes and odour of unwashed bodies hanging in the stale air, served to create an eye-watering atmosphere.

The bones of the animals and birds the men had eaten were burned in the fire, helping to save precious fuel; the men's own waste was thrown with that of the horses and fire ash down the steep mountainside. That all created more than enough man scent around the area to be sure no mountain lions would climb up to the cave.

The men had gotten tired of playing cards and rolling dice in the stale atmosphere, betting for Lucifers, roll-ups, baccy and cups of rotgut, or even just piles of stones. There was an occasional argument and some mild face-offs, but Carlin was soon able to restore order. His hard manner and sharp voice quickly stopped any quarrel in its tracks. They all knew only too well there was no alternative to being holed up in the cave.

Vince Lange mostly watched their goings on silently from his books, sometimes he'd join in with the card games, putting up with their taunting and sneering comments about him being a 'Preacher man.'

He was listening, biding his time, watching, learning anything he could about the men. All the time, everything he saw and heard was being stored away in his very good memory, to be fetched out and used, should it be needed, at some time in the future.

Lange was acutely aware that any small thing he could discover about any of them may well be very useful to him. He was also acutely aware that anything he might unwittingly give away about his true self, would get him killed, instantly.

The hideout was one hell of a dangerous place for Vince Lange to be in for so long, but as he was part of the gang now, he had no choice other than to be there. Anything else would have gotten him killed anyway. Frank Carlin had the blackest, iciest of hearts. Lange knew that full well. He'd seen it first hand, often enough.

Suddenly, the fragile peace was shattered. A fight broke out between One-eyed Jack and Benson. Jack leaped to his feet, hand instinctively dropping for his gun. Too late, though, he remembered Carlin had all the guns in the strong box, which he was sitting very firmly on top of right then.

'You callin' me out, Benson?'

'Don't be so stupid, Morten, we don't got no guns, do we, you idiot?'

'Nope, but we damn well got our fists!'

Benson leaped up to face his accuser, each man wound up like a rattler ready to attack. They charged at one another like wildcats, their bodies crashed together, kicking up dirt and gravel in clouds, snarling and snapping at each other viciously, both getting more and more bloodied.

Spotting an opening, Benson grabbed Jack around the throat with both hands, lifted him clean off his feet and rammed him hard up against the rough rock wall of the cave.

Jack Morten was kicking up the dirt, scratching and grabbing at Benson's hands in sheer, raw panic. The veins in his neck swelled, his face quickly started to change colour to dark purple and his single eye began to redden and pop.

Mendoza was laughing, egging Benson on, with a twisted, evil smile on his greasy face.

'You guys!' Carlin let out a shrill long

whistle. That didn't work. 'FELLERS! Guess you better give it up now, huh? Now!'

Benson turned to face his boss and almost imperceptibly let the grip of his hands loosen from around Morten's thick neck.

One-eyed Jack's feet made solid contact with the ground once more, his face began to change back to its normal colour, the veins shrunk back to their rightful size and his bloodshot eye returned to its proper place. Mendoza stopped laughing and sidled off into a corner, hoping to avoid his boss's deadly gaze.

'He accused me of cheatin', boss!' Benson snapped, pointing an accusing finger at the still gasping Jack.

'And were you cheatin', Jack?'

Their leader's voice was cold enough to chill the air in the warm cave. Jack bent over double, coughing and spluttering, hands to his neck, trying to get back his breath and composure. He knew all eyes were on him, but worse, Carlin's gun was still on him and waiting. Finally, managing to breathe almost normally once more, Morten shook his head painfully, stood up straight and replied in a ragged croak.

'The hell I was, boss! What's there to cheat for, a few pebbles and a smoke, for God's sake? I'd be plumb crazy to cheat for somethin' so damned stupid!'

A coughing fit shook his body and he rubbed at his bruised throat once more.

'And what do you gotta say, Benson?' Carlin drawled menacingly, waving the gun in the other man's direction.

'I saw it, boss, he slipped a white stone from up his sleeve, the snake!'

'I reckon you guys are going plumb stir crazy. Killin' one another over a pile of damn stones! What in the *hell*! You get to your bed rolls, settle in and damn well shut your flamin', yakkin' traps, the pair of you. *Now!*'

Carlin shook his head and sneered at the men in disgust as he waved his gun at them. Both immediately went, with their heads down like chastened children, to their respective corners. They sat there, glaring at one another and across at their boss, muttering and cursing under their breath.

Jack was still rubbing at his throat and coughing occasionally. Carlin stood there, the gun still in his hand as he looked down at them, shaking his head almost in despair.

Vince Lange could see the cracks beginning in the little group at last and he sighed with relief. This was exactly what he'd been waiting so long for. Now he decided it was high time to stick a wedge into that crack and give it a push. He made a suggestion.

'Boss, sure looks like some of us could do with a taste of fresh air for a change, huh?'

Carlin spun round to face him, gun poised. He stood over Lange for long moments.

Lange met his stare like for like and smiled slowly, whilst at the same time holding his breath. The silence in the cave was intense.

'Just sayin', boss, is all.'

Lange shrugged and smiled crookedly

at his boss, hoping his smile looked convincing, before he returned his gaze casually to the book he was reading.

Carlin didn't smile back at him; he hardly ever smiled. Slowly the gun lowered, and he pulled a wry face.

'Yeah, son, guess you could be right. Been a long while trapped in here this time, ain't we, fellers? Guess we're all goin' a tad stir crazy, huh? The animals could sure use some extra exercise, I reckon.' He turned to the rest of the men. 'Mebbe the kid's right. Could be a good idea for us to get out in pairs, go scoutin', see if we can find some more provisions. Per'aps we could find us some no-name town, or a ranch we ain't hit yet!'

Skinner and Mendoza laughed hoarsely, Jack snorted in agreement and made sure he got his comment in fast.

'Sounds good, boss, I vote me and Benson go out first.'

Carlin didn't miss his quick, snake-eyed glance across at Benson.

'Oh yeah? So you can kill one another just as soon as you hit flat ground? I reckon not. Skinner and me can keep an eye on you two bastards for a coupla days, 'till you cool down; Mendoza and Lange can go out first and bring us back new supplies. If'n they can find any damn place we ain't hit yet, that is. OK! Get going you two. Now!'

Lange wasn't best pleased about being partnered with Manuel Mendoza; the two of them didn't get on well at the best of times, and he reckoned that was probably why Carlin had done it. He was putting them to the test; he was always testing out his men in one way or another.

Still, Lange couldn't really complain, he'd been the one who'd voiced what they were all feeling. To make any complaints now would just cause more ructions within the ranks. He quietly packed up his saddle-bags and went to tack up his grey, closely followed by the Mexican.

After they'd geared their animals up, Carlin handed them their weapons, then, kitted out for the bad weather, the two men headed down the tunnel to the cave mouth. The closer they got down towards the entrance the colder the air became, until both they and the horses were breathing out clouds of thick white steam, even before they opened the final gate to the outside.

Lange held on to the horses as Mendoza tried to shift the gate. It was blocked solid with snow and ice so he couldn't budge it. Lange ducked under the horse's bellies to go to Mendoza's aid and after a whole lot of grunting and cussing between them, they finally managed to loosen the grip of the thick, white blanket on the door.

They prised it open, just about wide enough to enable them to push away as much of the soft fresh fall of snow as they could. Then they struggled to get the horses and themselves out of the cave and on to the path at last.

As they left the cave, both men automatically raised their hands to their eyes; the stark, searing brightness of the large expanse of snow was dazzling. Snow blindness could be a real problem if they didn't somehow shade their eyes, until they became more accustomed to the vast field of gleaming whiteness.

Mendoza gave a long, low whistle as he looked around, squinting from under the wide brim of his sombrero, shaking and blowing on his hands in an effort to warm them up again.

'Whew, it sure comes down in the night, huh, Preacher?'

Lange looked around; Mendoza was right. Jack had been out hunting only two days ago, and come back with three mountain hares, but there wasn't much trace left of his tracks out there now. In those two short days, another heavy snowfall had wiped out just about all marks and features of the landscape around them. It would make the trip down to level ground pretty damned difficult, even dangerous.

They tied bandannas across the horse's nostrils to protect them from the harshest of the bitter air; then both men pulled the collars of their thick sheepskin coats up high, heaved their mufflers right up to their eyes and set off.

Lange let Mendoza lead the way to start with. He'd been with Carlin the longest and was the right hand man, if anyone could find his way down, Mendoza could. Lange didn't like the Mex much, but the man sure knew what he was doing around the cave area and Lange respected that.

The horses shook their heads, snorting loudly as the cold air hit them; the men shivered. It had been much warmer in the cave than either of them had realized and the stark reality of the harsh temperature outside had just kicked in.

Slowly leading their mounts and silently giving thanks for the fact that the snow, for a while at least, had stopped falling, the two men made their cautious way down to the fissure. It took way longer than either of them had expected to reach the flats.

Mendoza had to keep clearing the path in front of them with a handful of sticks, to allow Lange and the horses to follow more easily. Lange couldn't go forward and help him, there was no way he could get past Mendoza's horse to reach the front, he had no idea where the path lay under all the thick, soft snow, and one wrong step on the steep track would have been a disaster.

By the time they had all reached flat ground, both men and animals were already panting heavily from the exertion of the climb down through the cold, glistening covering.

Picking out the track hidden under the snow, then finding the way through the loosely strewn boulders and rocks which littered the area, had been difficult. Lange knew he would have struggled if Mendoza hadn't known the way down as well as he did.

The going from there on in would be tough for the men and even harder for the horses. The snow reached above the animal's knees and being so fresh it was still soft, not hard packed, so with every step they took they sunk into it near enough to chest height.

The animals had to lift their feet up high in an attempt to plough some sort of path through the freezing blanket. It was hard, tiring work for both the men and their mounts.

'This rate, it'll take us nigh on a week to find some sorta town. That's if'n we don' freeze to death 'fore then! Whose stupid idea's this?' muttered Mendoza bitterly.

Lange ignored Mendoza's pointed remark. He too, was beginning to regret his suggestion that they should get some fresh air. Even the rank smokiness of the cave would have been marginally better than being partnered with the crazy, knife-loving Mex in this weather.

'Maybe we'll strike it lucky and come across a ranch, eh?' he said.

'Huh! I don' think there ain' no ranch close by. I done been roun' here nigh on five year, ain' never see no ranch yet.'

'Is there any path you haven't taken before?'

Mendoza looked around, trying to take in any landmarks that he might be able to recognize, it was difficult with everything sheltering beneath a cushion of gleaming snow. Eventually, he pointed roughly in a south-westerly direction, frowning and shaking his head.

'Ain't been that way much. 'Ees all rocks, dried up riverbeds an' diamond-backs last time we rode it. Boss say ain' no point goin' that way no more, wouldn' be any *hombre* in his right mind settlin' out there.'

'Well, what say we give it a try now, eh? There won't be no diamondbacks about in this stuff. Who knows, maybe some no-brain greenhorn settlers might have landed up hereabouts since then. Or, could be there's some Big-horns wandering about. Hell, we can't just go back empty-handed, can we? Carlin'd roast us alive.'

'Huh. Sure would, evil bastard that one, ain' he?'

On that one point, at least, they were agreed. Mendoza shrugged, hawked and spat a stream of dark brown chewing baccy, which froze solid almost before it hit the ground.

'Yeah, OK then, Preacher man, we go that way, Carlin ain' watchin', I reckon we try.'

The Mex turned and plodded off in the direction he'd pointed. Lange sighed, shook his head in dismay at the situation he'd talked himself into; then followed close on Mendoza's tail. The going was painfully slow, both animals and men were already becoming tired.

Thick lumps of ice were clinging to the horse's tails, manes and forelocks. Every time they or the men lifted their feet, it looked as though they were wearing thick, white boots. Any hair the men had left exposed was quickly covered in a layer of shining white crystals. Every breath they breathed out froze and hung in the air in front of them.

Their boots doubled in weight with the cold, clinging mass, making it twice as hard to lift their feet. At almost every step, the two men stamped their feet to try to dislodge the snow. What little progress they were actually making was wearying.

The dark was closing in on them fast now. It was beginning to look as though they'd have to hunker down with the horses in a snow hole overnight.

Lange really wasn't too happy about that. Especially as, if that was to be the case, he'd have to get up real close and personal with Mendoza, if neither of them wanted to freeze to death in the night. That was a pleasure he'd rather not have any time soon, thank you.

The men had been taking it in turns to lead the way; the front man had the hardest job of ploughing through the deep snow to make a track for the man behind to follow more easily. It helped ease the pressure on the horses too.

The snow started to fall again, it was coming down ramrod straight, covering their tracks fast, layering a heap of white shining crystals atop everything in its track.

Mendoza was out in front, with Lange a few yards to his rear when suddenly the Mex held up his hand.

Lange pulled to a halt close behind him.

'What d'you see?'

Lange cupped a hand over his eyes, the

better to try seeing what might be out there, but everything was blinding white, fast turning to murky grey with the fading of what little daylight was left.

'I think I see a light dancin', up ahead aways. Ain' there now, though. Over there.'

Lange stared in the direction Mendoza was indicating but there was no light. The stupid, bloody Mex was going crazy. Lange shook his head. That was all they damn well needed.

After a few moments more of peering into the swirling snow, they carried on moving, looking about them as they trudged along, just in case there really was a light somewhere, and both men knowing they'd soon have to find some kind of shelter for the night.

'There! Look! Up ahead now. I tellin' you I seen a light. See it? There.'

Lange looked along the line of the Mexican's arm, trying to see through the tumbling flakes. It took a while, but eventually, he too spotted the faint flicker of yellow light. A lantern. That meant habitation. At long last! Maybe they could sleep in a barn tonight after all, not a snow hole.

Mendoza pushed on as fast as he could through the clinging, white mass. Lange sure hoped there wouldn't be any trouble with the rancher. Mendoza's temper was notoriously mercurial.

3

At last, they reached what appeared to be a small ranch. A crooked sign hanging above the hastily erected and badly crafted entrance informed them that the place was nothing more than a small, hurriedly built, rawhide outfit, grandly named as the Kicking J.

The two men made their ponderous way along the path toward the house. This close up to the place they could smell the wood smoke from the fire. The frozen, still air had meant there was no wind to blow the smoke away, it just hung like a swirling storm cloud above the house.

That was why they hadn't smelled it before now, ordinarily the wind would have blown the smoke towards them; they would have known there was a dwelling ahead of them and gone for it straight away.

There were a couple of well-trodden

paths around the small house, to and from the barn, the corral and the small outhouse. It looked as though whoever had erected the buildings was none too clever with his hands. There didn't look to be a straight line anywhere on either the buildings or the fences. They'd been put up in a hurry.

The house was lacking a proper veranda, a plank path lay close to the edge of the building and a small porch guarded the doorway. A weak yellow light gleamed from the small front window and a storm lantern hung flickering faintly above the door. The weary men tied their equally weary horses to the hitch rail; Mendoza looked around the place and sneered.

'Huh. This joint ain' no bloody good to us, Lange. Look at the place. They don' got nothin' we can use, 'ceptin' maybe a coupla old horses, an' a milkin' cow in that there barn.'

'Well, we'll probably be able to spend the night in that barn, at least we'll be warmer than out here and we'll be fresher for getting on our way again in the morning. You stay there.'

He stepped up to the door, Mendoza had tied the horses and was close behind him. Lange called out to warn the inhabitants before rapping on the door. The Mex snorted.

'Why the hell you worried 'bout scarin' 'em, Lange? Jes' go in, fer Chris'sake.'

'We're trying to get us a bed for the night, Mendoza. If we scare 'em, do you think they'll let us lay up in their barn? They'll most probably run us off with a damn shotgun.'

He heard Mendoza snort again as the door opened a crack. A middle-aged man peered out cautiously. Lange could see the primed shotgun in the man's hands as he warily looked them up and down through the narrow gap.

Lange pulled down his muffler to let the man see his face and put out both of his hands, palms upwards in front of him so the man could see he wasn't carrying. He heard Mendoza snort derisively behind him.

'Who're you, mister? What do you

want? It's one hell of a bad night for any travellers to be abroad hereabouts.'

He strained to see past Lange and quickly pulled the door even closer to him when, in the small, yellow light of the lantern, he caught sight of the rotund Mexican leering in at him.

'Sir, we were wondering if we could bed down in your barn for the night? We were headed for the nearest town, got caught in this here blizzard. Thank God we saw your lantern or we'd be in a hell of a state by now. We'll be off again by first light.'

The man frowned, but didn't open the door any wider. Lange heard someone in the house behind the rancher and tried to sneak a look, but the man just pulled the door even closer to him. He motioned with the shotgun.

'Go ahead, wouldn't leave a dog out in this. But you best get gone early, OK?'

'Sure we will. Thanks, mister, really appreciate it.'

Lange touched his hat in salute, turned to go to the barn and bumped right into

Mendoza, who was standing close behind him, trying to peer through the crack in the door. Lange stepped on the Mex's toes, and got a mouthful of abuse in both English and Mexican. The two of them jostled for position on the porch before turning and going back down the steps.

They heard the loud bang as the door slammed closed behind them and a fall of fresh snow dropped from the rough roof to land with a dull thud, right where they had been standing. They untied the horses and led them across into the small barn, unsaddling, feeding and bedding the exhausted creatures down, before taking off their own mufflers and heavy overcoats and settling themselves into heaps of straw with their bedrolls for the night.

Mendoza had been right, there were a couple of rangy horses and an old milk cow in the stalls, but there was just about enough room for their own mounts too. Neither man said much to the other, as they bedded themselves down and pulled their coats over their blankets for an extra layer of warmth.

Lange settled himself down; the journey had exhausted him. Both the straw and his blanket were warm, a damn sight warmer than a snow hole at any rate. The sounds of the animals gently chewing and shuffling, and the scent of the crushed straw beneath him were comforting.

His mind drifted away, he was asleep in no time.

He slept very deeply.

Lange was disturbed from his rest and groaned; turning over in the warm hay, he wondered what it might have been that had woken him.

As the waking eased itself down into his sleep-soaked brain, he searched his mind for something. What the hell had penetrated such a deep sleep and woken an exhausted man?

He looked around, owl-blinking in the darkness. Blast it, the dawn hadn't even broken yet. Lange strained his ears and tried to focus his eyes. There was a pile of straw beside him, a worn, crumpled blanket lay close by, but Mendoza was nowhere in sight. His mind began to put the signs together.

Then, a terrible choking scream seared itself deep into Lange's brain. That must have been what had woken him. Instantly, he knew what was happening. Damn that Mendoza!

Immediately, Lange was up and grabbing for his gun belt, buckling it on and clearing leather as he ran from the barn. The door to the house stood wide open. A small yellow light drew him towards it, as another loud scream shattered the dark silence.

'Mendoza! Where in the hell are you? You bastard!'

Lange knew what he was going to see when he entered the house. It had been a woman's scream, unmistakably. And he knew how Mendoza liked to treat his women. He'd seen the Mexican's leavings way too many times before now.

His skin crawled as he reached the door. On the floor just inside the open doorway, thick blood pumping freely from a savage knife wound in his chest, lay the man who'd answered the door earlier, feebly gasping his way to his maker.

The dying man had just enough strength to point a trembling arm towards a back room before a stream of dark, sticky blood bubbled from his mouth and he finally collapsed.

Lange quickly stepped over him, knowing the rancher was way beyond any help he could give. He strode across to the door the rancher had pointed to, and heaved it open.

'Mendoza, you bastard! What the *hell* d'you think you're doing ...? Aw, shit!'

The scene in front of him left absolutely nothing to his imagination. A grey-haired woman, probably the wife of the now dead rancher, was lying on the bed, tied hand and foot to the bed-rails with strips torn from the rags of her clothes. Those clothes that did remain on her were in tatters.

Lange's quick glance took in the fact that she was covered in deep cuts, some of which were bleeding profusely. Mendoza had been playing with his precious knives again. He was kneeling on the bed next to the woman, with one of his razor sharp knives gleaming cruelly in his hand. The knife, and his hands, were dripping with blood. His pants were half way down his legs, his hat and jacket lay in a dirty heap on the floor.

The woman's eyes met Lange's as he stood at the threshold. He saw the pain in her dark eyes and the terror with which she looked at him. To her, at that moment, he must have seemed like just another outlaw come to help his friend and take what he wanted from her.

She whimpered and thrashed about as much as she could, in a vain attempt to hide her half-naked and tortured body from Mendoza, and trying vainly to escape. She was fastened way too tightly to free herself, her ankles and wrists were already bleeding from her fierce struggles.

The woman's clothes had been hacked into rags and were strewn about the blood-soaked bed. Her mouth was stuffed with a piece of bloodied cloth and she whimpered gutturally. Pointedly, the Mex looked at the primed Colt in Lange's hand.

'Whad'ya think you're gonna do with that there toy, kid, huh?'

'Get the hell away from her, Mendoza! Or I'll blow your filthy head right off your damn shoulders!'

'Aw, Preacher, this nice lady an' me, we was jus' getting' ourselves acquainted. Ain' that right, Chiquita?'

He leered down at the woman, waving his bloodied hunting knife towards her face; desperately, she tried to pull her head away. Lange took a step forward, seething anger flashing from his eyes.

'You drop that damn knife and get the hell away from her, Mendoza. Now!'

Slowly, and without taking his eyes from Lange's, Mendoza climbed from the bed, pulling up his pants with a struggle. He fastened his belt and stood up straight, then he began hefting his knife from hand to hand, never once dropping it.

All the time the Mexican's dark eyes were blazing fiercely into Lange's with

61

a sneer of pure hatred and undiluted violence fixed on his lips.

'Happy now, Preacher man?'

'No. Now you damn well untie her. Quick.'

Lange motioned with his gun towards the woman. She lay silently, tears mixing with the streaks of blood on her cheeks, watching with wide, scared eyes as the Mexican sneered at Lange, shrugged his shoulders and casually fixed his clothes, without any apparent intention of obeying the younger man.

'What ya gonna do with her, Preacher man, huh? Wan' her for yoursel', yeah?' The Mex bent down, still not breaking their stare, and scooped up his jacket and hat. 'I already try her don' I. She ain't no good. Dried up ol' whore; way too ol' to be any use to a strong young feller like you.'

Mendoza placed his hat and knife within reach on the foot of the bed. Leering at the younger man, he picked up his knife and winked at the woman.

'Look, Preacher, how's 'bout you le' me

finish off some more with my li'l Chiquita here, then you have your turn, huh? I make sure she still got some life lef' for you, kid.'

Lange was silent, his mind in turmoil, he was seething with anger, his heart pounding, the blood boiling in his veins.

In order to save the injured woman, he'd have to kill Mendoza and take the woman into the nearest town. He couldn't go back to Carlin's gang after that and he needed to, no, he had to. He was too close to his goal to let it all go now, but he wasn't about to leave this woman to Mendoza's terrible games any longer.

Almost two years of hiding, of keeping his secret. Two whole years of planning, two years of getting so close to his goal, gaining Carlin's trust. Worse, almost two long and terrible years being involved in, and through that, condoning some of the worst atrocities he'd probably ever seen. Was all that about to be thrown away, just because the stupid Mex couldn't keep it in his pants? Lange swore loudly.

Mendoza laughed.

'Yeah, tha's it, Lange, you come on over here, kid, she ain' goin' nowhere. You help yourself. I wait.'

The Mexican trailed the point of his hunting knife down the side of the terrified woman's thigh, drawing a long thin line of blood from the soft flesh in its wake. She flinched, squealing loudly through the gag. Mendoza laughed harshly.

'Oooh, I like when they squeak, don' you, Preacher? Like a leetle bird singin', eh?'

Lange levelled his Colt at Mendoza's head and cocked the hammer. His heart was pounding but his hand was rock steady.

'Untie her, Mendoza. Fast!'

'Or what, kid? Huh? What you gonna do?'

The Mexican frowned, shrugged and then grinned crookedly at the younger man.

'Or you're a dead man in about ten seconds, you bastard. One?'

Mendoza shrugged again and smiled

slowly. Lange saw the blackened stumps of the other man's teeth and the leering smile as Mendoza ignored him and went back to his earlier position, kneeling on the bed beside the woman.

She was lying in terrible silence, struggling to breathe through the gag, tears rolling down her pale cheeks, awaiting whatever fate these two men had in store for her.

The Mexican leaned forward with his knife to cut the strip of cloth tying one of the woman's thin wrists to the bed. Suddenly, moving way faster than Lange would have believed possible for a man of his size, Mendoza sunk the knife right to its hilt in the woman's chest, with a loud and sickening thud.

Quickly, he swung right round on the bed, pulled another knife from someplace about his person and hurled it towards Lange.

Shocked into silence, Lange instinctively ducked, and as he did so he felt the knife slice into his arm as it tore past him, before it finally crashed to the floor. At the same time and without hesitation or conscious thought, he pulled his trigger.

The Mexican's face disappeared in a cloud of gun-smoke and a splattering of blood. He fell forward, clutching ineffectually at his head. At such close range there wasn't a hell of a lot of his head left, his motions were simply those of a dying animal in the last throes of its life.

Mendoza slumped sideways and fell slowly from the bed, to lie almost at Lange's feet in a sticky, spreading pool of blood. Lange leaped over the sprawling body to go to the aid of the woman on the bed. As he reached her, however, he could already see that it was too late.

Mendoza's large hunting knife had gone in deep and the woman's life was draining away fast, along with the blood pumping thickly from her chest. Lange could hear her breathing, ragged and gurgling through the cloth stuffed in her mouth.

She looked up at him in a silent plea, the light fading fast from her dark eyes.

Quickly he pulled the gag from her mouth, unfastened the ties and pulled the heavy quilted bed cover over her naked, damaged body. He didn't want Mendoza's cruelty to be the last thing she would know on earth. Gently touching her pale face and wiping away her tears with an edge of the cover, Lange whispered close to her ear.

'Ma'am, I am so sorry, I wish I could have saved you from this — from him. Your man's waiting for you, ma'am. You rest in peace now.'

The woman's eyes flickered open. He could see the life ebbing from her thin, tortured body as she tried to reach a shaking hand out to him. He took hold of her small, cold hand in both of his and held on, squeezing tightly. It was the only comfort he could give.

She opened her mouth to try speaking. Her voice was so weak that Lange had to put his ear close to her mouth in order to catch what she was trying to say to him. He could hear the air bubbling in her blood-filled lungs as he did so. His eyes filled with tears.

Her breath whispered through his dark

hair and Lange's own breath caught in his throat as he leaned in towards her.

'*Th-h-ank — you — hh ...*' she sighed.

Her head lolled back and her hand lay cold and slack in his. She was gone and Lange was angry as hell. Mendoza had killed two innocent people and done God knows what to this poor woman before killing her. What the hell for?

Lange's one small consolation was that the Mex now lay dead at the foot of the bed. He would never understand men like Mendoza, causing pain and despair wherever they went. What the hell was the point?

Swiping hot tears from his eyes, Lange stood up and went to go and check on the rancher, even though he was sure there was nothing he'd be able to do there.

Cursing loudly as he tripped over the Mexican's body, Lange aimed a hard kick at it. A sudden sharp stab of pain in his arm made him aware that Mendoza's knife had caught it as it had whizzed past him.

He looked down at the blood seeping

through his shirt and running down his arm. Ripping a strip of cloth from one of the bed sheets, Lange tied it around the cut. It wasn't too deep, he was strong, it should heal well.

Luckily, he'd taken his heavy coat off and left it in the barn; he'd be able to protect the cut from the worst of the weather with that. Leaving it open to the freezing cold could cause it to become infected.

There was no way he'd be able to bury these good people, though, that was for certain; the ground would be frozen solid and way too hard now for him to even get a shovel in. That saddened him. He wouldn't have bothered to bury the Mex anyway, the son of a bitch really wasn't worth it, but the rancher and his wife, well, they deserved a burial of some sort. It was the right thing to do.

On the up side, at least it had sorted out one problem for him. Now he could go back to the cave hideout with his secret still intact.

Lange slumped on to the old rocking chair that stood by the bedroom door and held his head in his hands, thinking hard. Deeply disturbed at the outcome of the morning, he was filled with serious doubts about the sense of what he was really doing with Carlin and the gang.

Right now would be a real good time to just run off and leave them to it. Would his conscience allow him to do that, though?

He sat on the rocker for what seemed like hours, juggling with his thoughts, trying to work out the best way to go from here.

Eventually Lange stirred, looking around the place almost as if seeing it for the first time. He frowned deeply and stood up, shaking his head.

'*Damn Mex*,' he muttered under his breath as he moved around the place, opening cupboards and drawers.

There was only the one way he could see out of this predicament now.

There was only one way he could see to keep in with Carlin, keep his secret and make sure there would be no comeback from the gang.

4

Later that morning, Lange rode slowly away from the ranch, leading Mendoza's mount and the two farm horses. He hadn't bothered to tie them together, knowing they wouldn't go far from one another in the deep snow; as herd animals they'd all keep pretty close together.

He'd untied the old milk cow; she'd either wander off and find food and shelter somewhere, or die of cold before she was found. No point taking her back to the hideout, what the hell would they do with her, except slaughter and eat her on the spot? He had more than enough on his hands with the three laden animals now trailing behind his own.

As he headed back for the cave, following along the rough tracks he and Mendoza had made earlier, Lange glanced back over his shoulder only once.

The flames had taken a strong hold of

the place by then and were dancing up high into the cold, grey, early morning. They were casting an eerie red and orange glow wide over the brightly gleaming snow, staining it with dancing streaks of bright colour.

Smoke hung black, thick and steady above the house, with no breeze to carry it away. The roof was already on fire and beginning to tumble in; sparks were dancing and riding high on the plume of hot air. The ash was landing like dark grey snow, in a dense layer on top of the white mounds around the house.

Lange had carried the old man into the bedroom then wrapped him and the woman together on the bed under the heavy patchwork quilt. He said a short prayer over them and asked their forgiveness.

Then he had gone all round the house and taken everything he thought might be of any use to the Carlin gang. All the provisions, cans and packets, sacks of grain, blocks of hard cheese and sides of dried or salted meat went in the pile.

Reluctantly, he took almost all the

things the couple had set by to see them through the long, hard winter. No sense in leaving them behind to burn, not when the gang could make good use of them. He took some of the man's clothes and a couple of thick blankets from a large chest at the foot of the bed. As he closed the chest, he saw a name painted on the lid. That name burned itself into his soul at that moment — *Levin*.

He came across a smaller chest under the bed which contained a shotgun, two handguns, boxes of ammo and two hunting knives, all of which were too good to leave.

Lange then went over to where the Mexican lay, surrounded by a congealing pool of blood. Unfastening the man's heavily ornamented gun belt, Lange pulled it from him.

He took the three knives he found about Mendoza's body, along with the one he had pulled from the woman's chest, once he knew for sure she was gone. He also picked up the one Mendoza had thrown at him earlier.

The Mexican's sombrero was still lying on the bed — that too went in the pile; then Lange pulled off Mendoza's boots with their heavy, sharply rowelled spurs. He needed to be able to prove the man really *was* dead when he reached the gang again. No man would part with his boots, not unless he was dead.

Lange didn't even bother moving Mendoza from the place where he'd landed.

There had been plenty of rope out in the barn, so, using some of the bedding from the house, Lange parcelled up and spread the provisions and other goods equally between the two farm horses and Mendoza's dun.

He took his time in tying everything up tightly, fastening thick strips of sacking over the animals' nostrils. When they were loaded up, he secured each animal to the hitching rail. There was no rush. He knew no one else would be coming anywhere near this godforsaken, ramshackle place in such bad weather.

Lange had reluctantly taken the lantern

down and scattered some of the fuel across the bed and into each room of the small cabin. Finally, he smashed the lantern on the floor just inside the door. Glancing around one last time, he pulled a Lucifer from its block and struck it as he stood in the doorway. Then, stepping quickly out of the house, Lange dropped the match right into the wreckage of the lantern.

Instantly, a bright ball of orange flame exploded upwards. Lange jumped away from the house and unhitched the animals, pulling them quickly away from the flames, watching for a while to be certain the fire had taken a proper hold.

When he was sure there was nothing anyone could possibly do to put out the flames, Lange mounted his horse. Pulling his muffler up to his eyes, he took the reins of Mendoza's dun and headed back towards the hills, and the life he had unwillingly made for himself.

It was a long hard ride, but the journey was just a little easier this time, because he was travelling back in the tracks he and Mendoza had made on their way out. Luckily, there had been no fresh snow since last evening to cover the trail.

Lange prayed it would snow again once he'd reached the hills, to hide his tracks. With four heavily laden horses, there was a deep, wide trail behind him now, one which could easily be followed by almost anyone.

It seemed as though luck was on his side; the heavy, dark grey clouds were thickening, and lowering, becoming heavier and more oppressive. The air now had a strange, almost greenish-yellow tinge to it, a colour which he knew heralded another weighty snow-fall. Lange also knew he had to push on hard if he was to reach some sort of shelter before the snow reached him.

He'd seen animals and men trapped in snowfalls. They froze stiff, real fast. They died where they sat, or stood. No amount of warm clothing could prevent that harsh, freezing, cutting air from getting right inside a man's bones, fixing an iron grip on his innards, until he turned into an icicle. That was not the best of ways to die.

Sooner than he would have expected, Lange saw the approach to the cave appearing through the gloom ahead of him. Thank God he wouldn't have to spend the night in a snow hole with four horses at least. He heaved a sigh of relief.

Lange didn't really want to spend another winter holed up with the Carlin gang either, but there wasn't any choice, not yet, not now he was so close. He'd just have to sit it out one more winter and hope like hell that he could finish the mission this time.

It had already been way too long. He needed to get back to normality soon, before he became as twisted as those men.

Mentally hitching up his pants and steeling himself for the welcome he knew would be way less than friendly, as he was returning alone, Lange headed up the winding path towards the fissure.

Dismounting part of the way up the track, he fastened the reins of each horse to the stirrup leathers of the one in front, to ensure they would follow, and also so that they could walk in single file up the narrow, steep path.

Leading his grey horse, Lange proceeded upwards with caution, just in case there was a lookout posted anywhere. Squeezing round the Devil's Elbow, he began to relax. The snow wasn't far behind him, but now, he was safe. For a while.

Reaching the entrance unchallenged, Lange started to pull the roughly built door aside. As soon as the opening was wide enough, he pushed the horses past him into the tunnel and whistled loudly to let those inside know he was back.

As the last horse plodded wearily past him up towards the cave, Lange replaced the covering to the entrance behind them. Turning to follow the horses, he saw the figure of One-eyed Jack up ahead, reaching out to take the lead horse.

'Lange, you're back early. Where the hell's Mendoza?'

Jack's voice was little more than a growl, as he looked behind Lange and saw he was alone. This would take some explaining, but Lange had spent the time on the journey back to get his story straight and he had Mendoza's belongings with him to back it up.

'Where's Carlin?' Lange replied sharply.

He certainly wasn't going to tell this particular story more than once.

Jack led the horses into the cave where the men were lounging around, but they got up when the laden animals came into view, grabbing at them and unloading the packs, taking off their gear and fastening them up with the other animals.

Carlin remained sitting in a corner, back against the cave wall watching everything, a thin, dark cigarillo hanging loosely from his bottom lip. He eyed up the animals, watched the men unpacking all of the supplies, then turned his attention to Lange.

'Sure fetched us some interestin'-lookin' trade goods there. Horses ain't up to much, but I reckon if'n we get stuck, they'll make a fair stew, eh? How'd yuh come by this lot then, kid?'

He slowly unfolded himself and got to his feet, looking around. Lange knew he was looking for Mendoza.

'We found us some shelter in a small ranch late last night, boss, then — well — let's just say Mendoza and the owner, they didn't see eye to eye about things.' He shrugged.

''Bout what 'things' was that exactly, son?'

Carlin's voice was slow and hard. Mendoza had been riding with him a long time.

'A woman.'

Lange looked hard at Carlin. The two men stood, eyes locked, for what seemed like long moments until the spell was broken by a shout from one of the other men.

'Here's Mendoza's boots boss, and his hat! And here's his gun belt.'

'Well, I guessed you wouldn't believe he was really dead, not unless I fetched some proof back here for you to see,' shrugged Lange.

Jack passed the greasy sombrero over

to Carlin. He examined it, there was no blood on it, the Mex hadn't been wearing the hat when Lange had shot him, but the boots and gun belt passed over to Carlin were covered in blood.

All the men recognized them. They'd seen them often enough, no self-respecting man would part with either his gun belt or his boots, not unless it was over his dead body. It was sure and certain proof.

'Well, I guess he's gone then right enough. Shame. But you done well, Lange, fetchin' all this lot back here on your own. Looks like we'll have enough to keep us going for a while longer now, eh?' He nodded towards the group of men quarrelling over a side of dried meat. 'Hey! You damn well put that over in the corner with the other provisions, I'll say who gets what and when!' he shouted.

The men stopped their bickering and sorted out the bounty, placing it in piles around the cave. Carlin commandeered the thicker of the two blankets, passing the other one over to Lange, who took it reluctantly, remembering the woman.

He didn't really want it, but had no good reason to refuse, so thanked Carlin and threw it down in his own corner, shrugging off his jacket and dropping that on top of the blanket.

'So, this here woman then, kid, who the hell was she? And what happened to Manuel?'

Carlin's voice held a sharp edge of suspicion.

'Dunno who she was, boss.' Lange shrugged and looked at the floor, carrying on in a quiet voice. 'It was getting dark, and the blizzard was coming in real hard. We were exhausted. Landed up at some run-down ranch out to the southwest. Looked like real fresh settlers, boss. Mendoza reckoned you'd been that way before and there was no homestead there then.'

Carlin shook his head in agreement and motioned the younger man to carry on.

'Must have been real greenhorns, boss, to end up in a godforsaken place like that. I asked them for shelter. The old feller said we could bed down in the barn, but Mendoza went into the house while I was asleep. He killed the rancher. Looked like just one blow too, boss.'

He shrugged, trying to keep down the anger he was still feeling.

Carlin snorted and smiled, almost as if in admiration of the dead man's skills.

'Yeah, the guy sure was good with them there knives, eh? Go on.'

'I only woke up when the woman screamed. Hell, boss, you know how much Mendoza likes — liked, to play with the women. He's like a bloody cat playing with a mouse, enjoys torturing them some before he finishes them off.'

'Sure, I know. Manuel was a cruel one, but he was damned loyal to us — to me, so how come as you killed him, kid, not just over some useless old whore, I hope?'

The coldness in Carlin's voice was obvious, he and Mendoza had been riding together for years; Lange guessed they were the nearest things each one must have had to being family. He also knew Carlin was aware Mendoza and he hadn't got on well together. Lange had to be careful with what he said next.

'Nope, not that, boss. Wasn't me that killed him anyways. It was the rancher himself. Hell, boss, she was an old lady, could have been your mother. What he was doing to her, it wasn't right. Her old man found them. It all went crazy. Mendoza stabbed the woman in the heart, then threw another knife at the husband. It was mighty fast, missed him and got me as I went in.'

He rubbed at his arm for emphasis and just in case it might have gone unnoticed. Carlin stared at the bloodied cloth tied tightly round Lange's arm and motioned him to continue.

'The old man shot Mendoza point blank, right in the face. Then he turned the gun on me. I had to shoot the old guy, boss. Couldn't do anything else, sorry.'

Lange shrugged and looked at the floor again, hoping like hell that Carlin wouldn't think to question the series of events any further. It was a long time before Carlin spoke again.

'Sounds like you couldn't do nothin' else right enough. But I sure hope you gave Manuel a good burial, Preacher?'

That was it, the catch-out question. He'd been waiting for it.

'Couldn't bury him, boss, ground's frozen solid. I couldn't bring him back here, could I? Didn't want to leave him lying around there, though. I laid him out peacefully on the bed, took off his gear and said a few words over him. Then I packed up the old folks' provisions and set fire to the place.'

'And the old folk, what'd you do with them, kid?'

'Aw, I just left *them* where they'd fallen. What the hell else could I do, boss? They'll have been burned along with Mendoza. I made certain sure the place was burning really well before I left. I was just worried about making him comfortable, didn't really think much about what to do with them. Sorry, boss.'

Carlin leered at him. Lange supposed it must be a smile of sorts, but a cold chill crept up his spine. Living this pack of lies was beginning to wear him down and lies like that, even to Carlin, didn't help any.

'Hey, kid, don't be sorry, I reckoned something like that would come sometime, the way he was with women. Just seems a mite convenient is all. Guess we can't dispute the proof, though,' he frowned as he fingered the conchos on the Mexican's bloody gun belt thoughtfully, 'I reckon I'm gonna be needin' a new second any time now, eh?'

He looked around the cave, the men were still checking out the provisions Lange had fetched back with him; they were going through the piles on the floor, arguing over the weapons. Carlin sat wearily down on the box of guns, lit himself another cigarette and studied the men for a while, as Lange stood beside him quietly.

'Y'know, kid, you could've just taken Mendoza's body into the nearest town, gotten the reward and cleared off outa here. He'd a damned good price on his head. Why the hell didn't you do that?'

Lange hadn't expected that one; he had

to think fast.

'Well, hell, boss, there's money on *my* head too! The sheriff would have taken one look at the posters and I'd have been slapped in a cell there and then. Anyway, this here place is my home now. You guys, you're like my family. Where in the hell else would I be going?'

That last stuck real deep in his craw, but he hoped he'd sounded sincere, as Carlin subjected him to that hard stare once more.

'Yeah. Well, I guess I'd have done the same. Anyway, you did real good, kid, bringin' this lot back here yourself, through this weather.'

'Thanks, boss.'

Lange relaxed at last. His story had been accepted, for now. He was still part of the gang, unfortunately.

He went over and started helping the others place the loot into the niches reserved for the different items. There were jars of preserves, tins of meat, sacks of flour and dried beans, sides of dried smoked meat, oil for the lamps. He'd even found a couple of small casks of whiskey, which raised a fiery debate as to when they should be drunk.

Before he'd fired the house, Lange had reluctantly emptied the rancher's pockets of the few small coins he carried and a pocket watch. He'd also taken the few small items of jewellery he'd found in the woman's dresser drawer. He didn't think they'd have much value, but needed to bring back some personal possessions to prove his story.

There had been a locket in the drawer, he'd taken that too, and now, as the items were being passed around for the men to check out, he had a chance to look at it properly at last.

It was made of some silver-coloured metal he didn't properly recognize; it looked as though there had once been a coating of enamel over it. There was delicate filigree work on the front and the back was rubbed almost smooth, as though it might have been worn often.

Inside, there were two miniatures, one was of the man whom Lange recognized as the husband, and the other was of a young, fair-haired woman.

Not the wife. Not unless it had been made when she was much younger. But why would she carry her own likeness around her neck? Maybe it was a daughter. Lange felt ashamed of himself for taking their personal possessions, but at the same time, he knew it would have been expected, so to keep his secret safe, he'd done it.

Now, though, he hesitated over the locket. It pricked his conscience for some reason.

'Boss? You mind if I keep this trinket?'

He asked the question as casually as he could, as he lifted the locket. Carlin took it from him and examined it closely. He tossed it back with a grunt. Lange caught it easily and waited for the answer.

'Ain't gold, nor even silver far as I can see. Prob'ly tin. OK. You keep it. Is it a gift for some little dove we ain't heard about? C'mon, kid, why'd you want a worthless trinket like that?'

Carlin leered at the younger man. The

others were all silent as they turned to watch, waiting for his response.

'Well, hell, boss, if I take these miniatures out of it, I've got a real pretty gift for any girl. It's likely to get me some extra special favours, I reckon. Know what I mean?'

Lange flashed his boss a broad smile. The others laughed and whistled coarsely and turned to carry on with their work. Carlin studied Lange closely and silently. Lange wished he could figure out what was going on behind that cold, steely stare.

'Well, kid, you're a popular one with the ladies all right, I guess you could be right about the extra favours; keep it and good luck to you.'

Lange nodded his thanks as he pocketed the locket. The picture of the blonde girl, along with the memory of the name on the chest, had got him thinking. Maybe he would find her, somewhere, someday; make up some story about how he'd found it and give it back to her.

Maybe she was living in one of the nearby towns? Was she still Miss Levin?

He had a feeling that somehow he needed to make some sort of retribution for what had happened to that family, no matter how small it might be. Even though it hadn't been his doing, he'd had a big hand in what had happened.

Of all the things he'd seen and done since he'd been with Carlin, that was the one which pricked at his conscience the most.

Lange joined in again with the work of placing the items into storage, but every so often, he'd glance round and notice Carlin watching him with that cold stare once more.

5

The following morning, Lange took his turn on breakfast duty and brewed a fresh pot of coffee. He could feel by the tingles in his spine that he was being watched all the time.

He knew Carlin had his suspicions about what had happened; he also knew the boss would be working things out in his devious brain, trying to find out just exactly what else Lange was hiding from him.

If he did find out, well....

The cracks were widening now and Lange was pushing at them. At long, long last.

After breakfast, Carlin called them all together.

'I been thinkin'. We can't stay holed up in this here place like rats for the whole goddam winter. We're all goin' stir crazy already. I reckon we gotta break on outa here, head for some town we ain't hit yet and stick around there 'til spring. That'll give us a chance to check the place out and find the weak spots. Come spring, we'll hit 'em, real hard, real fast, and head back here again. Whaddya think?'

He looked around, waiting for an answer. He was the boss, it didn't matter a toss what they thought, they'd not go up against him. Whatever Carlin said, that was what they'd do. They all nodded and mumbled agreement.

Then Lange spoke up. He really wasn't happy with that suggestion.

'Boss, won't the sheriff have the dodgers for us all? How the hell are we going to get away with settling in any town hereabouts?'

'We keep our heads down and our noses clean, kid, that's how. We tidy ourselves up, separate into two groups, go in there a coupla days apart, book in at two different places, and don't do nothin' to draw attention to ourselves. Who the hell's gonna look sideways at two or three fellers goin' about their business in this weather?'

Lange was concerned, the nearest town to their hideout that they hadn't hit on yet was Pine Creek; unfortunately, it was also a place where he was known and he certainly didn't relish the idea of the gang hitting on anyone he knew. But how in the hell could he get out of it?

He could point Carlin towards Hickory Lake; that was a couple more days' ride in the opposite direction. Pine Creek was nearer, though; he doubted Carlin would want to risk an extra couple of days on the trail, not in this weather. Carlin voiced his very thoughts then.

'There's only the two towns we ain't hit yet, I reckon they're a touch too close to this here place for comfort, but the further afield we go, the harder it's gettin' to get back here in one piece. Looks like it's headin' for the time when we try to find ourselves a new bolt-hole, huh? Anyways, this time we gotta hit either Hickory Lake or Pine Creek. I reckon Pine Creek's the closest, 'bout a day's ride, so we'll go for that.'

94

Lange still disagreed.

'I reckon we should stick it out here a couple more days, though, boss; give us chance to grow beards and such, try and disguise ourselves a tad first,' he offered.

Carlin chewed on his baccy, thinking deep, while the rest waited. Lange knew such a flimsy disguise wouldn't hide him much if they did try to hole up in Pine Creek. But it might help for a while.

'Well, I guess the kid's right, maybe we need to make some sort of attempt at hiding behind some facial hair. The dodgers I last saw showed us all clean shaven, 'cept Mendoza, and that don't count no more. If'n we all grow beards, or 'tashes, or jest bigger beards, eh, Benson? Mebbe that'll help some.'

The men laughed. Benson and Carlin were the only ones who already had some facial hair but more of it wouldn't hurt any. Carlin went on:

'Yeah, that way we'll all blend in better. See, boys, now that's what comes of all that there book learnin', makes your brain work harder, you get to seein' things from

95

a different view than the rest of us, eh, Preacher? I like the way your brain works, kid. OK, we stick around here another week or so, then we head for Pine Creek. And we've got to settle on what names we're goin' to take too. Can't go in there under our real names, huh?'

Carlin settled back on his blanket and pulled his hat down over his eyes. That was the decision. That was the last word. Like it or not, they'd all be going to Pine Creek.

Lange would really have a challenge then.

Two weeks later, Carlin split them off; he would go first with Morten and Skinner. Lange and Benson would wait another couple of days and then follow the others in to town. They'd make out they were all strangers, but after a day or so they'd meet up over a drink and discuss their plans.

They'd all have to try and look for some kind of work whilst they were in the town too. Given the weather, it would be at least a couple of months, maybe more, before they could make their hit and ride back out.

Meantime, they didn't want to do anything to attract attention. They'd have to watch out for one another — too much drink, an argument over a game of cards; anything untoward which would draw the attention of the townsfolk would have to be kept in check.

As far as Lange was concerned, he could have done with a complete change of appearance. An unkempt, bushy beard and his long, wavy hair tied back in a leather thong wouldn't really do much to disguise him from those people who did know him. His dark eyes were bright and intelligent; they attracted a fair bit of attention anyway, always had.

He certainly didn't relish the idea of living at Pine Creek and trying to remain incognito for so long.

Carlin called Lange over to him and took him to one side; Lange knew there was something big going down as Carlin glanced around to make sure he wasn't overheard.

'Kid, I'm givin' you the chance to earn your place as my second. After the rest of us set off, you gotta get rid of Benson. He's way too easily recognized, what with the missing fingers and that damn squashed up nose of his. That there quick-fire temper of his is gonna get us all killed one day too. You do what you gotta do, Lange, if'n you ride into town alone, and bring me the proof he's dead, then you got the job. I like you, son, you work hard and you got an education, that's a damn good combination for a second. Whaddya say, kid?'

He slapped Lange on the shoulder, leering at him, with what Lange guessed was supposed to be a smile.

'Thanks, boss, I wasn't expecting that. Sure, I'll do it. No amount of facial hair's going to disguise him, fingers missing and all. He's got it coming anyway. You can count on me.'

Lange really hadn't been expecting this particular turn of events, and wasn't too happy with it, but he knew he'd be expected to look eager at the chance, so he tried.

'Oh, I know I can count on you, kid. I know I can. Be seein' you in Pine Creek in a coupla days then.'

He winked at Lange, turned and crossed over to the horses.

Carlin, Skinner, and One-eyed Jack Morten packed up two of the spare mounts with enough provisions to last a couple of days, and headed off. Lange and Benson watched them leave, ploughing a track through the fresh fall of snow.

When they reached the flat land, Carlin and Jack turned around in their saddles, and saluted the two watching men; then the three headed slowly off into the rolling, bright white landscape.

Lange and Benson pushed the hideout gate closed behind them and as they turned to go back into the cave for a couple more days, Lange was already working out in his mind how best he could carry out Carlin's orders.

The next two days were uneventful; the two men wandered around and carried on with more or less normal living in the confines of the cave. It was a hell of a lot quieter with only the two of them, and there were only three horses left now. It took some getting used to at first, but Lange knew he couldn't do anything about taking Benson out while they were still in the cave.

The day came round soon enough when they were ready to leave their shelter and head towards Pine Creek. Lange still had no idea what he was going to do in order to carry out Carlin's instructions. Anyway, they had to get out on to the trail first.

They closed the cave door, marking their territory beside it as usual and started down the perilous path to the flat land, Lange letting Benson take the lead. Benson obviously believed he was going to be the next man to take his place beside Carlin, so he reckoned he should tell the younger man what to do. Lange was happy to allow that; for a little while at least.

They led the horses down the almost invisible path and across the rocky area at the base of the tall mountains. To try riding them down the track would have been suicide. With the snow as deep as it was, one wrong step and they'd be straight over the edge. Men and horses panted with exertion. Their breath hung freezing in the air, as they picked their way down.

It was heavy going, even though they knew roughly where the path was, the lead man still had to find it under the deep, crisp, white blanket that was covering everything. Benson knew the track fairly well, but even he hesitated in places; the snow had wiped out almost all of the landmarks, and some of his turns looked to Lange like sheer guesswork.

They reached the flats without injury at last and paused to get their breath back. Squinting around, Benson whistled low and blew on his fingers; even through thick leather gloves, the extremities soon felt the brunt of such bitter and biting cold.

'Hellfire, it sure came down the last few days, didn't it? Can't hardly even see the tracks from Carlin and the others now.'

The landscape, for as far as they could see, was covered with a thick, rolling, shining white mantle. It hid all the rocks and fissures, softened the jagged lines of the mountains, and filled in the tracks the others had made on their way out. The snow completely disguised the state of the rough ground they'd be walking on. It was beautiful, but it was deadly as any snake.

It would be a damned hard ride to get to Pine Creek through all that. Normally it was about a day's ride to the town, which was why they hadn't hit the place yet, too close for comfort, but now, with the going as hard as it was going to be they'd have to make a camp on it for at least a couple of nights.

Lange knew it wasn't going to be comfortable. Especially considering that last order Carlin had given him.

Getting his bearings, Benson led them off in a general north-easterly direction. The going was tough, light snow was still falling and the air was bitterly cold.

Before they'd gone far, despite wearing hats, heavy coats with collars pulled up high, mufflers and bandannas doubling as masks around mouths and noses, any hair still showing had built up into a crust of white ice.

They tied thick strips of sacking to the horse's nose-bands, to hang down over their nostrils and prevent the harshest of the icy air from affecting their breathing. Even so, there was a covering of ice and snow over the animals' heads, ears and backs. A layer of ice had quickly built up on the sacking as their breath condensed and froze on the rough fabric.

The horses were struggling to make headway through the rolling, frozen covering. They were lifting their legs higher than normal to try moving forward, their feet sometimes jarring on the ground which was closer than it seemed through the white blanket.

The small group couldn't move at anything more than a slow walk, there was no way they could have gone any faster in that so it was a damn good job they weren't being chased.

It began to grow dark whilst they were still in sight of the mountain hideout, the journey was so difficult and slow. Lange knew it could take them up to a week at this rate to reach Pine Creek. The snow was deep and still falling. If the two men had been praying for a thaw to ease their way, they were well out of luck.

Ahead of them, they could just about see a familiar stand of old pines through the swirling grey and white murkiness. They headed for the trees; at least they would give the men a touch more shelter for the night than bivvying down in the open would.

It seemed to take hours just to reach the ragged, misty tree line and as they pushed into it, the temperature rose just a little. The wind didn't feel quite so biting in the sparse shelter of the old trees, and there were some small patches of sparse grass where the snow hadn't quite reached for the horses to eat. The two men broke out their bedrolls and makings of a meal. Benson looked around for dry tinder, whilst Lange unsaddled and hobbled the three animals.

A small stream wound through the trees, it was frozen, but still not too thick at the edges to break with the hard heel of a boot. They drew enough to fill a billy and their canteens; the horses drunk their fill, then went back to a patchy area of grass.

Huddled round the small fire later, each of them clutching a mug of strong, hot coffee, with their blankets wrapped tight round their shoulders, the two men watched the flickering embers in silence. Benson broke that silence.

'How d'you reckon Carlin and the others are doin' then, Preacher?'

'Well, I guess if they keep their heads down and don't go causing any trouble, they'll be fine, nobody's going to look too closely at them, I don't reckon.'

'Hope not. If'n they've been found out, you know they'll rat on us, don't you? Then we'll ride on in there and there'll be a goddamn neck tie party waiting for us.'

'You reckon Carlin would rat us out then?'

'Mebbe not Carlin, no, but that Skinner, hellfire, he'd damn well be the first to squeal if there was a reward at the end of it. I reckon it was a real wrong move to split us up like this.'

Benson spat into the embers of the fire for emphasis. The sparks jumped high into the green darkness around them. Lange snorted.

'Hell, man, if he ratted us out they'd surely look closer at him, then he'd be joining us on the gallows. Come on, Benson, you know this was the best way. They'll be looking for six men, not a group of three and two more riding in a week later. You're paranoid.'

'Well, if'n I knew what that there thing was, mebbe, but I just can't help thinkin' is all. I got me a real bad feeling 'bout all this.'

Lange huffed, he had a bad feeling about it all too, but maybe for different reasons, given the task he'd been given. He threw the dregs of his coffee on to the fire, damped the embers down some, stood the pot close to the embers to keep warm, and settled in for a cold and uncomfortable night, wrapping his blanket tightly around him.

He pulled his thick muffler round his ears and mouth and rammed his hat down hard over his face. Just a few moments later, Benson followed suit.

'You mark my words, Lange, ain't no good gonna come out of this here trip,' Benson muttered in the darkness.

He didn't know just how true that statement was.

6

The sound of the horses shaking the fine layer of ice from their backs woke the two men, who reluctantly left the warmth of their blankets. They built up the not quite dead embers of the fire, and brewed a fresh pot of coffee, all without saying hardly a word to one another.

Later, hitting the trail once more, Lange's mind was filled with their target town. Would he be recognized? Should he make himself known and swear them to secrecy? How, and when, could he best rid himself of Benson? How could he stop Carlin and the others from carrying out their plan, come the spring?

He reckoned he had about a day and a half left to sort out his problems before they reached Pine Creek. He knew he needed to act soon.

Riding into the town with Benson still alive and his prisoner, would attract attention from the townsfolk. It wouldn't gain him any points with Carlin, worse, Benson would just rat out the rest of the gang, especially Lange himself, within minutes of them being slung in a cell. Lange knew he couldn't allow that to happen, so he considered the alternatives.

Riding into the town with the dead Benson, which had been his first thought, would still attract attention, albeit of a different kind, but it would probably win him the trust of Carlin. In the very dangerous game he was playing here, he really needed that trust.

Although, in that scenario, too much investigating into Lange, or rather, into that man he had now become, would only bring other problems. He could just kill Benson of course and leave him out in the open, for the wolves and buzzards to finish off his sorry carcass.

Lange knew though, in that case, he'd have to give Carlin the proof that Benson was, indeed dead. Any damn way he looked at it, he really did have to kill Benson. Soon. That was something he really wasn't looking forward to.

The man had given him no cause, and Lange had never yet shot a man without reason.

He watched Benson's back, as the man struggled to blaze the featureless white trail ahead. Lange wasn't a coward, he wasn't about to shoot any man in the back. He'd have to call Benson out. And he'd have to do it quick.

Benson's voice broke loudly into his thoughts.

'Don't reckon we'll get much further today, Preacher, looks like there's one humdinger of a blizzard headin' right this way. We'd best find us some shelter, pronto.'

Lange looked where Benson was pointing. Sure enough, a huge, shapeless, almost black form was pouring like water down the side of the high mountains they had recently left. Folding and turning back in on itself, the thing was heaving like some enormous living thing, rumbling loudly and rolling directly towards them.

Benson was right, this was going to be a bad one and they could see it would be hanging around for some time. They needed to get a move on, get to some kind of shelter fast.

Up ahead a way there was a low outcrop of rocks and boulders. If they got a spurt on, they might just about reach that before the storm hit. It would provide at least a little protection from what they both knew was going to be a killing storm. Even just a little protection was way better than being caught out in the open in what was to come. They urged their tired, panting animals onward.

Reaching the outcrop at last, they quickly pushed the horses into a hollow, leaving their saddles and blankets on to help keep the warmth in and hurriedly fastening more blankets over the animals' heads and hindquarters.

The men could feel the temperature around them dropping fast. As the storm grew closer, a freezing wind began to spring up, the bitter forerunner of the real storm to come.

Quickly, the men grabbed their bedrolls and blankets, threw themselves to the ground, backs turned to the oncoming storm and lay there, huddling tightly together. They pulled both blankets over themselves for extra shelter and held on tight to any crevice they could get a grip on, as the storm roared in.

It surrounded them with noise and freezing, driving snow and ice. It shook the ground around them, howling across their crouched bodies, for what seemed like hours. It took their breath away, and with it, the chance of any kind of conversation, until the loud rumbling eased and the wind began to drop.

The horses had turned to face the rocks, with their back ends to the vicious storm. Their heads were hanging down low, as they tried to make themselves as small a target for the bitter wind as possible.

There was a thick layer of snow covering the animals and the two men, when they finally poked their heads out from under their blanket shelters, like turtles from their shells.

Benson was the first to make a move. He struggled to dig himself out of the snow hole, shaking the frozen coating from his clothes, blowing on his hands and pulling the blankets from the horse's backs and heads.

'Hellfire, but that was a close one. Two minutes longer gettin' in here, we'd be stiff as corpses out there. Damn it to hell, we'd *be* corpses,' Benson snorted.

Lange struggled to clamber out of the snow-covered shell behind him and looked around.

The sky was periwinkle blue, and clear as a bell in the direction the storm had come from. They could see it moving, like a dark and dangerous beast, tumbling and rolling its way into the far distance, laying down an even deeper layer of thick whiteness in its wake.

It was heading directly towards Pine Creek.

The deep tracks the two men had made to reach this point were now completely covered; the way ahead would be even more difficult from here on in.

Lange was cursing his hesitation. If he'd finished Benson off before the storm, the man's body would have been hidden under the snow blanket until at least the spring thaw.

Lange wasn't comfortable with the task he'd been charged with. Which was why he'd been hesitating up to now. He knew damn well he couldn't afford that particular luxury for much longer, though.

The two men eventually mounted up and once more began to plough their way through the crisp, soft snow, toward their target. Lange was up in the lead this time. They were moving even slower than before through the freshly fallen layers of deep whiteness.

They stopped around noon to rest and feed both themselves and the animals, neither man talking much to the other. Both were thankful the snow had stopped falling, for the time being at least.

As they were about to mount up once more, an all too familiar sound rang out, sharp and loud in the clear freezing air.

Benson was drawing a bead on him. Damn it! He must have known what Lange was planning all along. Slowly, Lange turned to face the other man, raising his hands as he did so. He frowned at the other man.

'What the hell are you doing, Benson?'

'What's it look like I'm doing? For a clever feller, you can be damn stupid sometimes, y'know, Preacher.'

'OK then, so why the hell are you doing it?'

Benson's answer shook him.

'Carlin told me to get rid of you before we hit town. Said he'd be makin' me his second if'n I did. Guess he's gotten fed up of you an' your goddamn preachin', huh, kid?'

'Put the gun down, Benson and listen. Carlin told *me* to kill *you* before we hit the town. Can't you see he's playing us off, one against the other?'

'Shoulda done the job earlier, I reckon, that last damned storm would've covered your body up real good.'

'Let me get this here thing right. Carlin said that if you got rid of me, you'd be his new right hand man?'

'Yeah, so?'

'Hellfire! He told me exactly the same goddam thing, you idiot! He's manipulating us both, can't you see that?'

'He's what us now? Quit your high falutin' talk with me, Preacher, it ain't gonna work. You're a dead man.'

'Look, Benson, we could settle this now without anyone getting hurt. We split up; I go back to Carlin, tell him I killed you and left you under the snow. You head off some place, change your name and stay away, we don't hear from you anymore. That way we both get to live. What do you say?'

'I say — why the hell can't it be *me* who goes back to Carlin? I been with him a damn sight longer'n you have, Preacher. You could just head off back to Fresno.'

Lange shook his head slowly.

'Can't be. It's got to be *me* who goes back to Carlin. I have my reasons. Come on, Benson, I'm damn well giving you the chance to stay alive here. If you *don't* take this chance, you don't live. Simple as that.'

Benson laughed, a low sound, which echoed in the crisp air around them.

'Think you're gonna win this then, do you, kid? If'n anybody goes back to Carlin, it'll be me, so you best just think again, Preacher man. I sure hope you got one of them there prayers ready for yourself. You're gonna be needin' it.'

Lange thought fast. Benson wasn't known to be the brightest star in the sky, maybe he could be reasoned with, talked round. Maybe no one would have to die this day. If he merely wounded the man and sent him on his way, the problem would be solved.

'If you're calling me out, Benson, at least give me the chance to defend myself; don't just shoot me in the back where I stand, like a goddam coward. You know I'd have done as much for you.'

Benson hesitated, thought for a moment and spat a stream of thick dark baccy into the deep snow.

'Yeah, I reckon you would at that, Preacher. OK then, let's just walk on over there aways, kid, and I'll give you your chance.'

Lange reckoned it wasn't much of a chance, his one Colt against Benson's two, but it was the only chance he had, and he was confident he was more than a match for the older man. Slowly, he headed towards a fairly clear area, mind working out his next move, then stopped, with his hands still up high and his back to Benson.

Only one man was going to walk away from this. It had to be Lange.

'Turn round, Lange, goddamn it. I ain't bloody well shootin' you in the back.'

'There's a mighty fine thought, but I've seen you do just that before, Benson, and more than once, remember.'

'Well, OK, mebbe. But not to any man as I'm ridin' with. Now, you just turn yourself around, Preacher man, real slow, keepin' your hands right away from your iron.'

Lange started to do as he'd been asked,

but before he'd turned right round, he suddenly dropped to the ground, rolled into the snow, cleared leather and fired every slug he had up at the other man.

Benson was taken completely by surprise.

He tried to fire, but dropped hard to his knees with a loud grunt and a shocked look on his face. There was a smoking hole right in the centre of his forehead, from which a deep red drop of blood began to spill and freeze as it reached the air, into an almost black blob.

The man hadn't even had time to pull out his second gun, before Lange had drawn his.

Benson had managed to get off a couple of rounds, but they'd missed Lange by yards. Now, Lange watched as Benson toppled slowly, face down into the snow. More snowflakes fell, silently and gently, into the space created by his body, partly covering him. No doubt at all, the man was a goner.

Lange quickly pulled off Benson's boots, gun belts and overcoat, reckoning another layer would serve to keep him warmer, then he kicked some more snow in over the body. The man wouldn't show up now until the spring thaw. There'd be no one riding this trail again until then anyway. Once the thaw set in, the buzzards and coyotes would finish off the job.

Taking the saddle from Benson's horse, Lange dropped it down beside the still figure of the dead man, after all, why the hell would a man be riding into town with two saddle animals? That alone would raise some questions.

He split the provisions between the pack-horse and Benson's mount, then tied the animals together and mounted his own horse, took up the reins of Benson's animal and set off. It shouldn't take him long now to reach Pine Creek.

Lange's mind was working overtime. Why had Carlin told both of them to get rid of the other? Had he hoped they'd both die? Didn't he trust Lange as much as he'd said he did? Had he found out Lange's secret at last?

No, if he'd found that out, Lange would have been well and truly dead, long ago.

This had just been a test, to see which of them was the strongest man. Carlin needed a strong man beside him, one who'd do just as he was asked, with no questions. This little task had just been another one of his tests of their loyalty.

Lange would really have to keep his wits about him from now on, because once he was in Pine Creek he would be in big danger, both from the gang he was riding with and also from some of the townsfolk.

Carlin didn't know it, but Lange was no stranger to the little town of Pine Creek.

7

Vince Lange rode slowly down the main street, keeping his head bowed until he reached the Silver Star hotel. He reckoned Carlin and the other two members of his gang would be lodging in the Painted Rose.

That was a combination of cheap hotel and mid-class whorehouse. Just the sort of place where they'd all feel right at home. As they weren't all supposed to be in town together, this plan was going to work better if the two groups of men were housed in different establishments.

The air was still bitter, fingers of smoke rose dark against the pale sky, telling of the fires warming interiors of shops and dwellings. Piles of dirty grey slush lay alongside the boardwalk, where the store keeps had swept it off the fronts, so the residents could walk a clearer path.

The wet and muddy street had been

carved into deep grooves where the snow was getting mushed and trodden into the earth. Within the ruts, the snow had melted into filthy puddles and frozen over again, only for the ice to be cracked and slivered into grey shards once more, when buckboards or farm wagons crunched through them.

There was a general air of weariness hanging over the whole town. It was going to be one hell of a long winter. Lange sighed.

He booked the three horses into the livery, unloaded them and stashed their tack. Then he went on over and checked himself a room in the Silver Star hotel, keeping his hat pulled down low and his chin tucked tight into his muffler as he did so.

He didn't recognize the desk clerk from his last visit and began to relax a little.

Settling himself into his room at last, Lange went over to look out of the window and along the muddy main street. He couldn't see any more of the gang around just yet, but there were plenty of people milling around the place.

The sheriff's office was just across the road from the Silver Star. The town had gotten busy since Lange had been here last, must have been about three years ago now. Surprising how things had changed and grown so much, in such a short time. He thought he recognized one or two faces, and sure hoped that they wouldn't recognize him in turn.

He figured he'd be OK for a while, though it was bitterly cold out there and everyone was dressed in their warmest clothes and mufflers, with their hats jammed down hard. They were mostly all going about with their heads down against the biting wind.

Hopefully, they wouldn't give him so much as a passing glance, but even if they did, the dark facial hair he was sporting should disguise him from them, for a while at least.

Lange was tired, the ride had been hard, and he hadn't realized just how exhausted he was. Throwing his hat on to the bed, he yawned loud and long, then rubbed his hands across his face and groaned.

It had been one hell of a long day; he reckoned it wouldn't hurt for him to have a lie down for a short while, before going to check out the town and meet with Carlin.

First, he hoisted his heavy saddle-bags up on to the bed. Opening up the flaps, he pulled out the contents, a change of underclothes, a couple of shirts, his shaving kit, baccy and various other possessions, which he placed on the table beside the bed.

Right at the bottom of one of the bags, beneath everything else he'd stored in there, was a small false flap. Invisible from the outside of the bag, it had been well hidden.

Lifting the flap carefully, Vince Lange pulled out a black bandanna, which was wrapping a small, hard object. He unwrapped it and gazed longingly at it. Of course it would still be there, but he had to check.

Smiling to himself, he re-wrapped

it and patted the item almost lovingly, before pushing it back under the flap and re-filling the bags.

A random thought hit him then, as he wondered if he might find Miss Levin, the one whose picture was in the locket he carried, here in town. He fished out the small pouch containing the locket and looked again at the picture of the girl. With a start, he saw her eyes looking straight at him, almost as if she was accusing him. Closing the locket with a sharp snap, he quickly replaced it in the pouch and pushed it back in to his saddle-bags among his clothes.

Lange placed the saddle-bags beneath the bed pillows, hung up his overcoat, hat and muffler on the pegs, tugged off his boots, then, still clothed, he threw himself down to sleep. It was a deep and almost dreamless sleep. He'd been completely exhausted.

The bright, late morning sun slashing across his eyes woke Lange with a start. He rubbed his gritty eyes hard. Looking around, he took in the room and his surroundings.

A small, scruffy room, but still, it was reasonably clean, it would do for the time he'd be here. The bed was lumpy, but not uncomfortable, hell, he'd slept in much worse in his time. He'd slept on the floor of a cave surrounded by Carlin and his men, for Pete's sake, and in comparison to that, a lumpy hotel bed was Paradise.

After he'd washed and eaten, he'd brave the town, see if he could hitch up with Carlin and the others.

Later, pulling his collar up high and his hat down hard, Lange walked quickly towards the Painted Rose to meet up with Carlin and the rest of the gang. Shifting his gaze about the place as he walked, Lange reckoned he spotted more familiar faces and hoped fervently they couldn't place him.

There was one face in particular, he was really hoping to avoid.

Entering the Rose, Lange ordered a shot of whiskey and leaned against the bar, casually looking around him. Over in one corner he saw Carlin and the others deep in a game of poker; none of them had looked up. He swigged back the drink, got himself another and wandered casually over to their table.

'Howdy, gents, mind if I sit in?'

Carlin looked up and looked around. He seemed surprised to see Lange there, not Benson. A chair was dragged over from the next table and the men moved round to make room for the 'newcomer' to sit in on the game, then another set of cards was dealt.

After some time playing, Carlin fixed Lange with his cold stare. Lange felt the full force of that stare go right through him, it was all he could do not to shiver, he knew he was looking pure evil in the eye. He could see Carlin weighing him up, deciding how best to proceed. Lange sat silently playing his turns, waiting.

'Ride in alone, did ya, mister?'

Carlin's voice was hard; he'd obviously been expecting a different outcome.

'Sure did. Damn lucky to make it here too. Got caught up in a real bad blizzard just a couple of days out. Lucky I found a good place to shelter. Nothing much would have gotten out through that lot alive.'

The comment wasn't lost on the men, who exchanged glances with one another, and looked over to Carlin who sat silently, studying his cards. Carlin couldn't just up and ask him outright. There were too many folks around who could hear what he had to say, they sure wouldn't waste any time in fitting two and two together and making a murder out of them.

'Where'd you come in from, mister?'

Carlin placed his cards and stared at Lange.

'Viper Creek.'

Lange placed his hand, meeting the stare like for like.

'Yeah? Heard they'd had a hold-up at the bank there. You hear anything 'bout that?'

'Not much, it'd been a couple of weeks before I got in there. Things were settling down some by the time I turned up.'

Lange went back to studying his hand and figuring his next move.

'D'they got any idea who done it?'

Carlin threw some chips in the pot.

'Don't reckon, they were scratching their heads a lot. To be honest, I wasn't listening to the tittle-tattle, just wanted to get going before the weather got too bad for travel. Know what I mean?'

He threw his chips in.

'Oh sure. I know real well, kid.'

That ice cold stare sent an involuntary shiver down Lange's back.

The next couple of hours were spent in card games. It was all too familiar for Lange to be playing hands with these men, but it was damned hard for them all, trying not to act friendly with one another so soon after supposedly only just meeting.

'Well, guess I'd best be off then, fellers. Be seein' you around, I reckon,' Lange said, as they finished a hand and he pushed back his chair to stand.

Carlin shot him a look then, which chilled him to the bone. He knew in that moment, no matter what he'd thought about being well in with Carlin and the rest of the gang, he was still dispensable. He'd have to watch his back while he was in town. The boss would think nothing of making up some excuse to get him killed.

Carlin wouldn't want to get him jailed, though, because then Lange would be able to tell the law all he knew about the gang. Nope, he'd certainly be killed, probably late one night, in some dark place on the outskirts of the town, in the most evil of ways imaginable.

Lange knew all too well, exactly what these men were capable of. After all, over the last couple of years he'd joined them on their raids, much against his real nature. Some of the things he had been witness to at those times were vividly re-lived in his nightmares.

He had tried always to keep himself apart from the worst atrocities as much as he could, without arousing too much suspicion. He deplored what he had seen and wished every day that he hadn't joined up, but he'd been given no real choice.

He thought he'd done a damn good job of blending in with them all up to now. Was Carlin's obvious mistrust simply because they didn't really trust a guy who buried his head in books, rather than join in their petty squabbling?

Whatever the reason, Lange knew he would have to keep his guard well up whilst they were all in Pine Creek. But later, when they'd pulled their heist and were running hell for leather from the town — what then? Run with them, risk them finding out about him and killing him later, or stick around town to be discovered, and take the consequences?

Hell, there was plenty of time to think about that later. They'd all have to stay here anyway until the spring thaw, like it or not. It was snowing heavily every day now and trying to run far in that sort of weather would be nothing less than suicide. Lange decided that he at least would try to find himself a job while he was in town.

Being busy would be a damn sight better than sitting around, drinking and card playing all day, and whoring all night. It was definitely better than worrying about who was behind him wherever he went in the town.

It would give him something else to concentrate on.

8

It didn't take long for Lange to find himself a job at the local feed merchants. He was weighing and bagging up feedstuffs, and carrying the sacks out to the wagons, when the local ranchers and farmers came in to collect their orders.

It meant he was out back, away from sight most of the time. Whenever he was called up to fetch out some feed and put it in a wagon, he made sure his head was well down. It worked pretty well.

Lange sometimes met up with the others in the Painted Rose for an evening; he felt he had to keep up to speed on their plans in order to figure out what his own plan should be when the time finally came.

They'd all been watching from various vantage points around town. Carlin, of course, favoured the Rose. He never attempted to find a job of work, didn't reckon he needed to. He'd brought along enough of their stash to last them all until the fair weather began once more.

Carlin preferred to sit in the saloon most of the day instead, sweet-talking the resident doves and wandering aimlessly around town, weighing up the possibilities for a heist, in between times.

Skinner had managed to get himself a job at the livery, cleaning out. He could remain anonymous there. Morten had found himself a real suitable job, as assistant to the local undertaker and gravedigger.

There were only the four of them left now, and Lange knew Carlin would be on the look-out for others who he thought would be fit to join the gang. He'd also be trying to decide who should be his new right hand man. The latter was probably going to be decided by how this heist went.

He realized for sure now, Carlin didn't really trust him, obviously hadn't for some time. Lange thought he must have let something slip at some time, although he believed he'd been careful enough around them all.

Still, he reckoned, there was no point in worrying over what had already been done. He threw himself into his job and waited for a signal.

One grey morning, Lange was called out from the back of the store to fetch some feed to one of the ranchers.

'Sure thing. On my way,' he replied.

Grunting with the effort, he heaved a bag up to his shoulders and walked out to the buggy. He dropped the heavy sack into it and turned to go and fetch the second bag. As he turned, he almost collided with a tall, well-built man. Lange side-stepped and apologized, keeping his head low, trying to get back inside without being recognized.

'Charlie! Charlie? Is that you?'

He froze. He'd done pretty well avoiding anyone who might know him up to now. But here stood just the person he really didn't want to see. The guy must have recognized his voice.

'Nope. Sorry, sir, name's Fletcher, John Fletcher.'

Lange had hoped he'd done a good enough job of disguising his voice, but it was obvious from the other man's tone and reaction that he hadn't. Now he'd been recognized. He'd just have to try and bluff it out.

'Well, hell, mister, you sure do remind me of someone I used to know.'

The man walked round him trying to look into his face, but Lange quickly pushed on and went back out to collect the second sack of feed. Damn it! If this guy really did recognize him, there'd be some awkward explaining to do.

'It is you, Charlie. It's me, Pete Mackie. You remember me. Sure you do.'

The man had followed Lange out to the feed store and was close behind him now. There was no way Lange could avoid a confrontation. He swung the second sack up on to his shoulders, trying hard to keep it between himself and Mackie; it wasn't going to work.

When he dropped that sack into the buggy and turned away to return to the comparative safety of the store, the other man stood full on in front of him.

'Charlie, come on, man, don't say you don't know me. Hell, I recognize you, even under all that face hair, what's that all about? You were always clean-shaven and real smart. Hell, I can see from your eyes that it's you. It's me, Pete. What's up? You lost your memory?'

Lange searched around in his brain. How best could he do this? Own up and swear the guy to secrecy, or carry on denying who he was and risk a very public argument? As he looked around, he cursed inwardly when he saw Morten standing close by, watching with interest.

Lange put his head down, pushing past the man into the back of the feed store. Mackie followed him, as Lange had hoped he would. As they reached the back of the store, he spun round and grabbed Mackie by the collar. His voice was low and urgent, as he tried to explain.

'Listen, Pete. Just shut up and listen. Yes, it is me, but you don't know me. You've never seen me before, OK? There's a real good reason, but I can't go into it now. I'll explain everything just as soon as I can. Meantime, you just forget about me, and don't mention seeing me. Not to *anyone,* especially your family. Do you understand?'

Pete struggled to get away from Lange, pulled his hands away from his jacket front and stood shaking his head. Lange's eyes blazed hotly and his breathing was harsh.

'Well, hell, Charlie, you look like shit, what's goin' on? What in the name of all that's Holy, have you gone and gotten yourself tied up in now?'

'I said, I'll tell you when I can. Now go, and for God's sake, don't you open your mouth to anyone else. Please?'

'If'n you say so. But you sure have changed, Charlie. What happened to that clean, smart, young feller you used to be, the one who....'

His words were cut short by Lange's hand clamped tightly over his mouth.

'Look Pete, just leave. Please. Don't speak. Go home to your family; forget you saw me. You don't know me any-more. You've *never* known me. OK?

I'm John Fletcher all the time I'm here. Understand? Go.'

Lange almost pushed the man out of the shed, following closely behind him as they went over to Mackie's buggy. Lange noticed Morten still standing nearby as Pete climbed up into the seat and took up the reins of the two matched greys.

'Thank you, sir, be seein' you again.'

Lange touched his fingers to his hat.

'Sure, sorry 'bout the mix up back there, Mr Fletcher. Be seein' you.'

Mackie touched the brim of his hat, flicked the reins and the buggy pulled away.

Lange heaved a sigh of relief as he watched Pete Mackie slowly drive away along the narrow, winding track, painstakingly created between mounds of snow outside the town.

He hoped he'd got away with it as a case of mistaken identity. As he turned to go back into the store, he saw Morten turn on his heels and walk briskly away. Lange knew he'd be going back to report what he'd just seen to Carlin.

Damn that Pete Mackie; he never could keep his big trap shut. Lange could only hope he didn't come across anyone else who recognized him. Equally, he hoped he really could trust Pete to keep quiet about his old friend being back in town.

Although, if one person had already recognized him, how long before someone else did? Someone else, who wasn't going to be half so easy to keep quiet.

He wandered over to the Painted Rose that evening, needing to know just what Morten had said, and if Carlin suspected anything. Carlin and the gang were all at their usual table when he walked over to the bar, and ordered his drink.

Lange stood looking around for a few moments whilst he downed the whiskey, then took another one across to the table. The men made room for him and he sat stiffly, waiting for whatever might come.

'Hear you's recognized today, 'Fletcher'.'

Carlin's voice was and low hard, as he stared at the younger man. Lange met

141

his stare, and the air around them grew noticeably colder.

'Case of mistaken identity, that's all.' Lange shrugged.

Morten dealt out a hand, Lange picked them up, eyes still holding Carlin's gaze.

'Yeah? Well, Jack here, he reckons that there feller knew you all right. Knew you pretty damn well too by all accounts. What you gotta say 'bout that?'

He placed his cards, and glared at Lange.

'I told you, mistaken identity. Never seen the guy before. I've never been in this here town before now. Hell, in this weather and all wrapped up like we are, it'd be damned easy to mistake one man for another.'

He shuffled the cards around in his hand, slowly lowering his gaze from that of Carlin's, so he could look at his cards. Lange held his breath.

'I guess you might be right. But you lie to me, 'Fletcher', and you won't be seein' the hideout again in this sweet life.'

The threat hung heavy in his tone. It

wasn't missed by any of the men; they glanced around at one another and frowned at Lange. He wasn't worried. He knew Carlin and the rest wouldn't risk tackling him in such a public place. Not until after the job was done anyway.

They needed to keep up a peaceable presence in the town, until the snow had melted enough to allow for a good get-away. Any altercation now would only serve to draw unwanted attention to them, maybe even get them slung in the town jail. Even Carlin wouldn't want to risk that. Still, the threat lingered around them.

They played on. Morten lost his hand and took off up the stairs with one of the dancing girls, leering back at the gang, as he followed her and smacked her hard on the backside. She squealed and giggled as they disappeared into the dark warren of bedrooms.

'Don't fancy a turn with one of the ladies then, 'Fletcher'?'

Carlin's voice broke into Lange's thoughts. He shook his head, grimacing at his boss.

'Hell, no. I can't say there's one here that takes my fancy any.'

He hoped he sounded believable. Carlin grunted.

'Well, now, you're still carrying around that pretty little trinket, ain't you? Surely, it'd buy you the favours of any girl you wanted? Is there one over at the Silver Star you've done taken a shine to? Young, hot-blooded *hombre* like you; I guessed you'd be lovin' yourself stupid by now.'

At mention of the locket, Lange felt a sharp pang of guilt, or perhaps regret, at the fact that he had the locket at all. Trust Carlin to remind him. As for giving it to any cathouse floozy, that really wasn't going to happen. He'd find the right owner, if he had to search the rest of his life for her. Somehow, he felt he owed it to that family to return it to her.

'Now that you mention it, there is a little filly over at the Star, but I'm aiming on taking it slow, get to know her a bit better, buy her a drink or two, you know? If I play my cards right, I could be in for some very special favours, know what I mean?'

He smiled broadly and winked at Carlin. After a long pause, Carlin's face slowly cracked into some resemblance of a smile that didn't quite reach his narrowed eyes, and gave him the look of a rattler about to strike.

'Sure, kid. You work it. I reckon that's one way. Bit too slow for my likin', though, how's about you, Sam?'

Skinner had been keeping quiet up to then. Now he looked at his leader, and then over to Lange. There was something in that glance which Lange couldn't quite place.

'Yeah. Hell, if'n I take a fancy to a tumble, first girl handy'll do me, none of that there pussy-footin' around. Takes way too long and costs too damn much.'

He and Carlin laughed together; then Skinner turned back to Lange.

'Still, I guess that's what comes from all that there book learnin', huh, kid? Teaches you all the wrong things, I reckon.'

Lange shrugged as the other two laughed and played their hands. He threw his money in the pot, played his own hand and lost. Thankfully at least that meant he could leave their company again. He picked up his hat and stood to leave.

'Remember, Lange, you lie and you die,' Carlin whispered harshly.

No one else would have heard him over the general ruckus, other than the men at the table; to the casual onlooker it just looked as if he was studying his cards.

'Sure thing, mister. See you around, fellers.'

Lange turned, shoved his hat down tight on his head and left the hotel with a definite feeling of discomfort prickling between his shoulder blades. He kept to the shadows, hoping there was no one else around who might remember him.

Luckily, the darkness was made all the heavier with the promise of more snow soon to come, and there weren't that many folk about.

Reaching the safety of his small room without being challenged, Lange threw himself on to the bed with a deep sigh. This was all getting way too complicated.

9

Pete Mackie turned up at the feed store again a few days later and nodded at Lange, as the feed was being loaded into his wagon. He followed Lange into the store again and out to the back.

'Come on, Charlie. Let me in on the secret. What in the hell're you up to here?'

He touched Lange's arm to turn to him. Lange spun round to face him, anger flashing like fire from his dark eyes.

'Look, Pete. Just leave it, will you? Please.' He took a deep, calming breath, sighed and continued quietly, 'I can't tell you, Pete, honest. People could get hurt. Killed even. You've got to know I don't want that. The less you know about anything the better. Trust me. You go back to your Rosie and the girls, and you tell them *nothing*. Not a word. You understand? Tell nobody anything, it's way too dangerous for everyone.'

Pete shook his head. 'Damn it, man! We were friends! We were real close. What's so secret you can't share it with me, for God's sake? Hell, what about our other friends? Come on, Charlie! You disappear for more than two years; then turn up here again lookin' like shit, telling me not to tell any of our friends you're here. Well, what if any of the others recognize you anyway? What you gonna do then, huh?'

'All I can say, Pete, is ... I'm sort of, well — in hiding, from someone who's here in town too. Don't ask any more, please. Aw, *hell,* I miss this damn place. I never reckoned I'd be coming back round here like this, though.'

The sigh that escaped him could have come from his boots.

'OK, buddy. I won't tell anyone. But you just take care y'hear, Charlie? If it's that damn dangerous, you take good care. Me and Rosie would sure like to have you over for a meal again sometime. The girls are growin' up fast, y'know, it won't be long before they got all the young bucks in the area after them! Best go and get the shotgun primed, eh?'

They laughed together, then Lange stopped and gazed off into the distance as he remembered his life before. Before he had joined Carlin and the rest of them. Before he'd become involved in their evil doings his life had been comfortable. He'd had friends then. Real friends, like Pete and his little family.

He sure as hell missed that life. Maybe it was about time now for him to settle some place, and he couldn't do worse than here.

'Look, Pete, come spring maybe I'll be able to tell you everything. Maybe I'll be able to get over to see Rosie and the girls then, but just for now you *really* can't tell them, or anyone else that I'm here. But especially not your family. OK?'

'Well, if it's so damn important to you, Charlie, sure, I'll keep quiet. Just you take good care of yourself. *Whatever* the hell it is you're doin' here.'

They clapped one another on the shoulders and Mackie left to go back home. Lange busied himself straightening up the feed sacks.

'Mistaken identity, my goddam backside.'

Lange swung round to see Skinner in the doorway of the barn, his hand hovering real close to his gun. How long he'd been there Lange had no way of telling. How much had the man overheard?

'Look, Skinner, that there feller's OK, he's a friendly guy. I reckoned it wouldn't do any harm for us to make friends with some of the locals. That way, we might find out something that could be of use to us later.'

Skinner snorted, turning his lips up into a sneer, obviously he didn't believe that story, he was primed and ready to drop Lange where he stood, right there and then.

'Yeah? Well, he looked like more than just a 'friendly guy' to me, looked like you two was pretty pally already.'

Skinner's hand moved dangerously close to his Colt and his eyes were narrowing to a squint as he spoke.

'You shoot me now, Skinner, and you know there'll be dozens of folk in here in no time, then you and the others will sure have some explaining to do.'

'Happen I'm willin' to take that there risk, Lange.'

'You might be, Skinner, but what about Carlin? You know damn well he'll drop you where you stand, if you stir up a hornet's nest round here right now.'

Their eyes locked and Lange could almost hear Skinner thinking over what he was going to do next. Lange himself almost held his breath, knowing only too well that if Skinner went ahead with what he was planning, all of the waiting and working, all that getting in with the gang and gaining their trust would be lost.

All of it would have been for absolutely nothing in that one moment.

Skinner dropped his hand from his gun and glared at the younger man. Still, he didn't move from the entrance, though, and Lange knew the other man was processing, working out what his next move should be.

Then a call broke the tension hanging heavy in the air between them, as the owner of the feed store shouted out, he was looking for Lange, or 'Fletcher', as he was calling himself now.

'Fletcher! Where in the hell are you? There's feed waiting to be loaded into this customer's buggy. Get your backside out here!'

'On my way!' called Lange.

He walked quickly past Skinner, out to the front of the store to find out what was needed. Chills ran down his spine as he walked away, thereby exposing his back to the man who was more than ready to kill him. Skinner would think nothing of shooting him in the back; he'd done it to others before, many times.

It seemed that this time, though, common sense won out. From the corner of his eye, Lange saw Skinner slinking back towards the Rose. No doubt he was going to report to Carlin.

Later that evening, Lange once more joined the rest of the gang at the Rose for a game of cards. They all looked up as he approached them. He'd got used to reading their expressions but tonight, all he could see was pure distrust from them all.

'Howdy, fellers.'

Carlin snorted and glared at him. The other two just looked back at their cards, shifting uneasily in their seats. Lange sat down and looked around at the men.

'What's wrong with you lot? You look like you're sitting on a bed of cactus spines.'

His attempt to inject some small vein of humour into the meeting failed miserably, none of the men cracked their faces. Carlin just glared with his narrowed snake eyes, as he weighed 'Fletcher' up and down, and said nothing at all for a long stretch.

When he did finally speak, it was in a low voice, without taking his eyes from the cards.

'So, 'Fletcher'. I hear as how you're makin' good friends with the locals, eh?'

'Well, yeah. I reckoned it would work out well, we get to know them, they feel easy with us and then they let things slip. Things that could probably help us out long term. I don't see what's wrong with that.'

He could almost feel the words sticking in his craw as he spoke.

'You've got yourself pretty pally with one of 'em in perticlar by the sound of it. What's he told you then? Anything we can use?'

Carlin laid his hand down.

'Hell, I've only just started talking to the man. Give me time, boss. Got to get to know the feller properly, eh?'

Skinner spoke up, his voice harsh and hard as he laid down his hand in turn.

'Sure looked to me like you'd got to know him pretty well out there, 'Fletcher', in fact, it looked like you's two were real old pals. What do you got to say 'bout that then, huh?'

Lange was growing uncomfortable beneath this cross-questioning. He looked across at Carlin and thought fast. His voice was barely a whisper as he quickly explained.

'Boss, you once said that because of my book learning, I thought differently to most other men you knew, yeah?'

Carlin nodded, stern and silent; Lange waited for Morten to lay down his cards before speaking again.

'Well, I'm using that different thinking to our advantage here.'

Lange laid down some of his cards and looked through the others he was holding. Head down, he carried on talking. No one outside of their small group would have been able to hear his low words.

'The way I see it, boss, is, if I get real friendly, real fast, with a couple of the folk here, they'll be fooled into thinking I'm an OK sort of guy. Then they'll let their guards down around me, let things slip, you know? I'll be one of *them*, a part of this town, see?'

Carlin laid his hand down slowly and looked across at Lange with a glint of interest showing in his steely blue eyes.

'Go on.'

'Well, I've already started telling folk how much I like it round here, how I'd like to settle down hereabouts. They're starting to trust me, boss, and I reckon trust's pretty important, if we're going to be stuck round here for a while, eh?'

He stared hard at Carlin. The older man matched his stare, and for a long moment, everything around them seemed to hold its breath, as Carlin thought over what Lange had said.

'See boys, now that's exactly what I mean.' Carlin looked around the table, with what approximated to a smile on his weather beaten face. 'You gotta get the trust of these here folks. The kid's right. Ain't I been tellin' you lot, book learnin's a good thing? Gets you to thinkin' about situations in different ways, 'stead of just chargin' in like a band of damn Injuns on the warpath!'

His smile was wide, as he looked around at them. 'Mebbe we should all learn from the Preacher here, and go get ourselves friendly with the locals.'

Morten snorted as he looked from Lange to Carlin and back.

'What? You mean not just talk friendly

to the ladies in here? You mean — huddle up to 'em *all?*'

'I sure do. It seems to be workin' for 'Fletcher', so yeah, let's all go get friendly with the locals from now on. No, not just the ladies, 'Mitchell', all of 'em. Talk more to *all* of 'em, men too, don't just hide in the shadows no more, get involved, make some friends.'

He looked around the men at the table again.

'Like the Preacher said, people will get to trustin' us more then. And trust's real important, ain't it? That way, they'll let their guard down round us and when we *do* hit 'em, they'll be so damned shocked, it'll take 'em longer to get up a posse, 'cause they thought they trusted us! Hah! I like it, Preacher. You done all right with your sideways thinkin'.'

Carlin laughed out loud, threw down his hand and grinned at the rest of the men.

Lange looked across at Skinner. He seemed as though he was about to burst. His face, or what bit could be seen of it through the hair, was turning puce. His tale-telling had backfired on him. Lange would have to watch his back even more closely now. Skinner wouldn't be past creating an 'accident' of some sort for Lange to be involved in.

'But, boss, how'd we get friendly with 'em?'

Morten seemed to whimper as he threw down his hand.

'Oh, fer God's sake! Don't you know how to talk to folk? Jest get talkin'. Talk about the weather; price of booze, state of the road, hell, any damn thing'll do. Cryin' out loud! Do I got to do everythin' myself?'

Carlin lost the game, threw down his cards and left the table, heading towards a small huddle of preening, dancing girls. He started talking to them and just moments later, he was following one up the stairs. He didn't throw so much as a backwards glance at the rest of the men, still seated at the table in an uncomfortable silence.

'Well, I guess that's me done then,' Skinner stated, throwing a losing hand down, and pushing his chair back to leave.

'Yeah, me too.'

Morten followed suit.

Lange was left sitting alone at the card-strewn table. He downed his whiskey in one gulp, and headed for the Star and the comparative peace and safety of his room.

10

The gang was some weeks into their stay in Pine Creek, and the weather had still showed no sign of easing up. Each morning, the storekeepers were faced once more with the onerous task of sweeping yet another thick layer of snow from the front of their stores.

Anyone who might be coming or going, to or from the outlying ranches, had the need to work in pairs and carry shovels along with them to keep their paths reasonably clear. No sooner had they cleared the way to get into town, than another snowfall covered up their tracks. It was wearying work.

Lange was getting on well in his job and so far, the only one who had recognized him was Mackie, so he figured he was doing OK. Skinner had started to talk more to the folk who had need to go to the livery.

Morten was kept busy helping to build coffins, mend wagons and any other jobs he might be asked to do. He was mostly stuck out at the back of the building, though, so he rarely had the chance to come into any sort of contact with many of the town's residents.

Carlin still wasn't working; preferring instead to gamble his days away. He reckoned a man with a belly full of booze would be sure to let his guard down. Ply them with liquor; play them in a hand of poker, loosen their tongues and that way, Carlin would be able to pick up information easily. Why the hell break your back if there was no need?

Lange had got into the habit of scanning the faces of any of the very few women he came across during his work. All the time, he was looking for *her*. He was looking out for that pale face, the one which stared out at him from the locket, accused, taunted; and sometimes, he felt, even pleaded with him to find her. His mind could find no rest.

Lange knew, only too well, the best

way round that was just not to look at the locket again. But it called to him whenever he was in his room. He tried to ignore it, but eventually he would find himself opening his pack and taking out the small pouch. He would sit and hold on to it for a while; trying to ignore the pull, knowing he should just replace it in the pack, but always, he had to open the pouch.

He would sit on his bed holding on to the locket; telling himself that the chances of finding her were worse than scarce and he shouldn't be looking at her again. And yet, always, like a rabbit hypnotized by a snake in the moments before a strike, Lange was drawn to open it. He'd grown to know the feel of the piece well by now, the slight roughness of the long chain, the patterns etched lightly into the metal, the small click as the lid unlatched, and the slight tightness as the two parts opened.

He'd noticed the hinge was bent a little, but didn't want to try fixing it. His big hands would most probably break it completely, so he took extra care in the opening and closing of it.

Then, when he finally opened it, there were the faces looking up at him. He'd grown to know them well also. The man; Lange would never forget how the rancher had tried to point him in the direction of his wife, trying his best to save her, right until his last breath. Maybe one day, Lange reckoned, he might find someone to love as much as that.

And the girl. Pale and smiling, high cheekbones, long wavy hair. His dreams were disturbed by the memories of that fateful day, and filled with visions of the flames, Mendoza's ugly face, and of the girl. His sleep was more restless than it had been in a long time.

Lange knew it was futile, that he'd probably never find the girl. Hell, he didn't even know if it was a likeness of the wife in her younger days, let alone a daughter, or sister. If it was the wife, then all the searching in the world wouldn't bring her back.

A daughter? She could be living

anywhere in this world; there had been no sign of any young woman around the untidy ranch house on that fateful day. Whenever he replaced the locket in his saddle-bags, and her face vanished once more, he would resolve again to find her, someday.

As he opened the window of his hotel room one morning, Lange noticed the first signs that a spring thaw was beginning. Where previously the long fingers of ice had hung in front of his window, almost obstructing the view of the town, now those same fingers were dripping.

There were just a few, slow, rhythmic drops at first. Then, as the sun moved higher day by day, and the heat of the days slowly intensified, the dripping also grew in intensity, until it was almost a stream of freezing cold water.

This was a good sign; it meant it wasn't going to be long before the whole gang could hightail it out of the place. It was also a bad sign, as Lange knew folk were going to get hurt. Probably killed, and some of them could be his old friends.

He knew he had to try doing something to reduce the future death toll. He also knew it would soon be time to inform the sheriff about what would soon be going down, in this usually peaceable little town.

That would mean exposing himself, though. He would just have to hope that the sheriff was the sort of man who would recognize and understand the truth of what he would be told. Otherwise, Lange himself would finish his days dancing at the end of a rope alongside the other members of the Carlin gang.

With the thaw beginning, the gang was starting to get restless. Carlin made them wait a while longer, though, knowing from long experience an early thaw could all too often bring a spell of even worse weather nipping at its heels. It would be damn stupid to make a move too soon, until they were certain the thaw was properly set in.

Lange was watching them all closely as he went about his business, he could see the cracks in their false personas beginning to open. He knew that, sooner or later, probably sooner, one or another of them would do something totally stupid. They were getting itchy britches — it wouldn't be long before the powder keg that was the Carlin gang exploded.

Lugging a sack of feed out for a customer one day, Lange saw Carlin himself watching. It was unusual to see him out and around the town, and Lange found himself wondering what the hell the man wanted. He dumped the feed in the wagon and headed back inside.

Carlin quickly stepped in behind him. Lange turned to see him standing in the opening to the feed store, arms folded across his barrel chest and frowning deeply.

'What can I do for you?' Lange ventured.

'Well now, 'Mr Fletcher', you can tell me if you've found out anything useful. Perticly about the bank. I know you've been in there. So, opening hours, where's the safe kept? Best day to hit it? Oh, y'know, just little, but important, things like them there.'

'Hell, boss, you know all of that as well as I do. Skinner and Morten have been in the bank, I reckon you have too, so I don't have anything new to tell you about it.'

Lange turned to get on with his work. Carlin suddenly appeared right beside him, a look in his eyes which, Lange recognized, spelled big trouble for someone. Probably him.

'Well, y'see. Me'n the boys, we've been watchin' you, Lange, real close of late. And we all reckon as you've been holdin' out on us, mister.'

'Holding out on you? How so?'

Lange pretended innocence, and gazed at Carlin with a frown.

'Now there y'are, see. You're one *damn* good liar, kid. Didn't have you down as lyin' t'me, though, not after all this time. You might be able to fool the others, but not me. You're lyin' 'bout somethin', an' I'm gonna find out exactly what.'

Lange heaved some sacks around while he thought about that comment. What did Carlin mean by saying he was going to find out? How did he intend to do that? The gang had nowhere to go. They'd be stupid to go causing any trouble now that they could almost taste a getaway.

'Listen, boss. I'm hiding nothing from you. We've all had to learn to be someone we're not lately, maybe that's all it is, maybe I just can't stop pretending, even around you guys.'

'Nah. S'more than that, kid. I seen you talkin' real friendly like to that feller as comes in reg'lar for feed. The one with the two greys pullin' his wagon. He came in town yesterday with his family. You know that? Didn't come in for feed though, did he? No. Did some fancy shoppin, all of 'em. That's a real pretty-lookin' wife he's got, yes sir, real pretty. And those kids, skippin' and laughin', young, soft, pink little ladies. I'd sure as hell like to get to know them two a bit better.'

Lange felt like he'd been punched in the guts; he gasped, clenched his fists and swung round, eyes blazing. He hadn't known Pete and the family had been in town the previous day. If Carlin or any of the others laid a hand on any of them …

'Listen! I told you, I'm not keeping any damn secrets. Why the hell would I? What good would it do anyone?'

Too late, he tried to bite back his anger. Carlin's cold stare burnt into him like ice, the smile on his face was wide and cruel. He nodded once.

'Yep. That's what I figured.'

Carlin swung on his heels and marched out of the store, leaving Lange open-mouthed. He knew in that instant, he'd given himself clean away, rounding on his boss as quick as that. Now Carlin knew that Lange was at least acquainted with Pete and his family, even if it was quite recent, and he would also know that very same acquaintance meant something to Lange.

Now Carlin had some leverage on the younger man.

Damn! Damn Carlin! That would teach him to keep his guard up around the boss. Lange cursed loudly and kicked at the door in his frustration.

When Pete came in for his next load of

feed and followed Lange out back, Lange rounded on him.

'What in the hell were you doing, bringing the family into town the other day? I told you to be careful! Damn it, Pete!'

He slammed his fist hard against the barn wall, not feeling the pain through the hot anger, which was burning him up. Pete stepped back. He knew his old friend was strong and now he was angry, Pete really didn't want to get in his way.

'What did I do? Rosie and the kids wanted to do some shopping. They haven't been into town for weeks. I couldn't stop them. How could I? That would have meant telling 'em about you, and about what you'd told me. I kept them well away from you, didn't I? Hell, Charlie, I don't want anyone to get hurt, but what was I supposed to do?'

He frowned and shrugged.

Lange sighed. It had been one hell of a long winter; the strain was beginning to tell on him, and there was still some time before the gang could try to get away from town. The weather was warming up and people were going about far less muffled up.

Sooner or later, he knew someone else would be bound to recognize him. Someone who wouldn't keep as quiet as Pete had.

'Hellfire, Pete! Didn't I tell you it was goddamn dangerous? Those people I told you I'm in hiding from? Well, it's not quite like that ... It's way more complicated. *Way* more. But they saw you all yesterday, now they've found out that you know me. Damn it! They're dangerous, Pete. You've got to be careful. Careful what you say and who you speak to, you've got to tell the whole family not to talk to anyone they don't know. Got it? Don't say anything to anyone, Pete. For God's sake.'

'OK, OK, but if Rosie wants to come into town, how the hell am I going to stop her?'

'Hell, Pete! Think of *something*. Try to keep them away until after....'

'After what?'

Lange shook his head and frowned, looking down at his boots.

'Nothing. I've said too much. Just go home, Pete, and keep th — no. Wait. Will you do something for me?'

'Hell, do you need to ask, Charlie? You disappear for years, and come back looking and acting like a wild animal! Knowing the man you were, something big's happening with you right now. And I can't say as I like what it's doin' to you. But sure, you know I'll help you, any way I can.'

Pete looked closely at his friend and saw a nervous, haunted man, with gaunt features, wild staring eyes and untidy hair, not at all the Charlie he used to know. Of course he'd help his old friend.

'Thanks, pal. Come back here tomorrow. Just you. I'll have something I want you to do for me, but you can't act too friendly with me. Anyone asks, and there *will* be someone who will ask, you only met me for the first time when I landed up here with the snow.'

He looked around to make sure they were still alone, and continued.

'My name's 'Fletcher' while I'm here,

Pete, Jack Fletcher, OK? Or Vince Lange to some. You've got to forget my *real* name. That's why, tomorrow, you can't bring the family here again. Just you. Meet me back here, same time. OK?'

He looked about him wild-eyed, as if something was hiding in the shadows waiting to pounce. Pete nodded and frowned, worried for his old friend's sanity.

'Sure, I'll ride in, say we forgot to pick something up if anyone asks. You take care, Charlie. I don't remember ever seein' you so het up. See you tomorrow.'

Pete left quickly. Lange sighed and sat heavily on a hay bale, head in his hands. This was getting difficult; he really had to take some sort of action soon. What he was going to ask Pete to do for him would just be the start of it.

After he finished work for the day, Lange went back to his room, sat down with a pen and paper and began to write.

11

True to his word, Pete turned up the next day riding one of his greys. Tying it outside the feed store, he headed round the back and went to where he knew Charlie would be.

Lange was taking an inventory of the remaining stock. He turned as he heard Pete approach, and looked all around, making sure there was no one watching, then drew his friend aside into the shadows and thrust a piece of paper into his hand. Pete pushed it quickly into his pocket without looking at it.

'Give this to the sheriff, just as soon as you can. But you've got to tell him not to make a move yet. Not until he gets my signal. Everything will be OK just so long as he stays calm. Understand?'

'Sure, he's to stay calm, not make a move. Wait for your signal. What the *hell* is going on, Charlie? Surely you can tell

174

me? We've known each other years; you know you can trust me.'

'Nope, because it'll show on you, won't it? Then the men responsible, they'll see you behaving differently and they'll know. Believe me, Pete, it won't be long now, I can see it. When it's all over, then I'll tell you everything. But not until then. Now go, but don't go directly to the sheriff, wander around, buy some sweets for the girls, look calm. OK?'

'Sure. But hell, Charlie, I can't say I like to see you looking this way.'

'I'll be fine. Go. See you around.'

Lange went back to his counting. Pete stood watching for a moment then shrugged, left the building and walked off down the street. He'd never seen his friend like this before. Charlie was behaving like a madman, seeing danger in the shadows, looking around as if someone was watching every move he made.

Pete really didn't like what he was seeing.

That evening, Lange joined the rest of the gang at the Rose. He had to keep up the pretence. It was more important than ever now. He looked around the table, noticing that Morten was missing.

'Howdy, fellers. Where's 'Mitchell' tonight?'

'Oh, he's just out doing a little errand for me.' Carlin grinned.

Carlin and Skinner exchanged a glance. Skinner dealt out another hand of cards, and they played on in silence for some time. Lange was well aware that it wasn't like Morten to miss a game, something was wrong.

He knew he couldn't afford to show his suspicions, he had to keep up the front, but his brain was working overtime. What in the hell was Morten up to?

'So, Fletcher. You learn anything new lately?' Skinner growled.

'Nothing since the last time you asked,' Lange retorted.

'You ain't learned nothin' more about the bank then?' Carlin's voice was quiet, filled with menace.

'What about the bank, boss?'

'I dunno. Thought *you* might. Seein'

as you're so damn pally with the locals an' all.'

'Yeah? Well we *all* agreed to get pally with the townsfolk weeks ago, didn't we?'

'Sure did. Sure did. Yeah.'

Carlin looked thoughtfully down at his cards, smiling. Skinner sniggered; a sharp look from Carlin cut him off short. They carried on with the game, but Lange was beginning to feel restless, there was something wrong, he could feel it. Where the *hell* was Morten?

Slowly, the answer grew in his mind, and it was all he could do not to leap up, turn the table over and run out of there fast. Instead, he gathered his thoughts, trying not to let the anger and fear show on his face.

He threw in his hand, yawned widely and feigning tiredness, he left the saloon, trying real hard not to hurry, trying to look as normal as possible, whilst all the time his whole body was crying out to him to run like hell.

Lange ran over to the livery; he'd had a gut feeling he knew exactly where Morten was. Saddling his horse, he lit out along the track towards Pete's ranch just as fast as his mount could carry him.

As he drew closer to the house, what he saw there, he'd sort of half-expected, but still it rocked him to the core. Morten's horse was tied up outside Pete's house. Skidding to a halt Lange leaped from his horse, flung the reins over the hitching post and headed up the veranda, steps two at a time.

He was dreading what he was going to find in the house. Bursting through the door, gun in hand, Lange was stopped dead in his tracks by the sight of Pete and Rosie sitting at the table, with Morten, who was looking mighty comfortable as he nursed a cup of hot coffee.

Lange glanced around, but couldn't see the children, they'd most probably be in bed by now, thank the Lord. A cold shiver of apprehension ran down his spine. What in the hell was Jack Morten doing, sucking up to Pete and Rosie like this?

Morten spoke. His voice sounded loud in the silence after Lange's entrance.

'Howdy, Lange. You always come into folk's houses thataway? It's sure as hell gonna get you killed one day, kid.'

'What the hell's going on here?'

Lange was confused. Pete spoke up quickly.

'Mr Mitchell here rode in about an hour or so back, from Viper Creek. Says the trail's clearing a fair bit now, he's looking for you, Vince. Some coincidence, eh? You both turning up here like this?'

That was it. He was blown. Morten would be sure to go back and tell Carlin how well he knew Pete now. Pete and the family were in danger. Although to give him his due, Pete was calling him by the name of Vince Lange, not using his real name, so he too must be aware that Morten meant trouble for someone.

'Bet you didn't expect to see me again so soon, huh, kid? Last we saw each other was Viper Creek, just after that big bank job, remember?'

Rosie poured Lange a coffee; he nodded his thanks and noticed that her eyes were wary as she looked up at him. Lange holstered his iron and sat at the table opposite Morten, glaring at him in undisguised anger. Morten took no notice at all and carried on talking.

'I was just asking Mr and Mrs Mackie here if they'd seen you passing through any time. They reckon you're workin' in the feed store in Pine Creek. Funny, that's just where I'm headed. How've you been, buddy? Long time, no see, eh?'

Lange was silent. His mind was twisting this way and that like a nest of snakes. What the hell could he do now? Killing Morten would bring Carlin and Skinner down on him faster than lightning. Not killing the man would endanger his friends and himself.

He glared at Morten with a cold anger that wasn't lost on Pete and his wife. Then he smiled stiffly across the table at the man.

'Sure, yeah, long time. What are you doing here?'

'Why, I'm jest looking for you, of course, Vince. I reckoned you might be close by; didn't get much of a head start on me before that weather came in, did you? Besides, I owe you something. I fully intend to pay *all* my dues.'

The coldness of that comment wasn't lost on Lange, nor on Pete and his wife, as they glanced at one another.

'You don't owe me anything at all, mister.'

'Oh, sure I do, kid. Remember? Me and Mendoza, we had a deal, didn't we? The next time we met up with you, we said we'd give you what was owing to you.'

At the mention of Mendoza's name, Lange stiffened.

'Mendoza owes me nothing, either.'

That name was damned hard to say through such a dry mouth.

'Oh, yeah. Yeah, he owes you a lot. Haven't you heard? Oh no, you won't have. Mendoza, he's dead now, so I'm here to pay his dues for him. Well, now that we're all here, Vince, why don't we ride into town together? You can direct me to the best flop-house and we can have a drink for old time's sake. Whaddya say, pal, huh? Oh hey, tell you what, Mr Mackie; why don't you come in to town with us, join us in a hand and a drink? I'm sure the little lady wouldn't mind?'

'Why that's sure pleasant of you, I ...' He saw the narrow-eyed look his old friend was flashing him and rapidly changed his mind. 'You know, I don't think I will. I'm plumb tuckered out, had a real heavy day. But if you're going to be around for a while, maybe I'll see you in town one day soon, eh?'

'Oh, you surely will, Mr Mackie. Very soon, I'm sure. Well then, Vince, shall we head off to town? Let's leave these good people to finish off their supper. We got a hell of a lot of catchin' up to do, eh, buddy.'

Morten left the table, and smiled down at Rosie, who smiled shyly back. Lange cringed, he didn't want this bastard wheedling his way into his friend's family. He stood quickly, pushing back his chair with a loud grating noise.

'OK, let's go. See you later, Pete.'

He almost pushed Morten towards the door, in his hurry to get him away from there. They said their goodbyes, then Lange and Morten rode off silently in the direction of town.

Lange was seething as he rode along. Was all his hard work going to come to nothing now, after all? What the hell had Pete told Morten? He could only hope he hadn't mentioned his letter to the sheriff.

'What the hell are you playing at, Morten?' Lange snapped.

'I don't know what you're talking about.' Morten leered round at him, feigning innocence.

'Getting your feet under their table. Why?'

'Well, hell, Lange, it was *your* idea, wasn't it?'

'*My* idea? How so?'

'Sure. Wasn't it you who sucked up to Carlin and said we should all go 'get friendly' with the locals? Well, that's just what I'm doing. I've seen the guy around town a fair bit now. Seen you chatting all friendly like to him. I reckoned he was a solid upstanding citizen; who's better to get to know, eh?'

Lange went cold. His own words had come right back to bite him hard on the backside. He hadn't thought any of the gang would actually do what he had suggested. To see Morten sitting at the Mackies' table, enjoying a brew and chatting to Rosie as if they were long-time friends really got Lange's anger burning.

'Listen to me, Morten; you *damn* well leave them alone. They're good people. They don't want some loser like you sucking up to them. And what was all that rubbish back there about Mendoza?'

'Oh. Mendoza, yeah. Well, now, he *does* owe you a lot, doesn't he, Preacher? He owes you, 'cause you gave him a good send-off, didn't you? And I know *exactly* the sort of send-off you gave him. So, yeah, I'm here to pay his dues. I've been watching you a long time. You don't fit with us, Lange.'

'Goddamn it, Morten! I've been with Carlin almost as long as you have! What the hell do you mean, I don't fit?'

'You heard me. I reckon there's something that's not right about you, Lange.

Can't put my finger on it, not just yet. But it'll come.'

He spurred his horse on. The town lights were guiding them forward now. Lange stopped his own animal and sat still, thinking. His mount began prancing and shuffling, it wanted to follow Morten's horse. Lange loosened the reins, pressed his mount's flanks with his heels; and it took off at a pace.

Lange caught up with the other man just at the outskirts of town. Morten didn't even look round as Lange arrived at his side, just kept up a steady pace towards the hotel.

Lange followed him into the town; but when Morten kept on going up the main street towards the Rose, Lange watched him go for a while, then turned and headed back for the Mackie place just as fast as his animal could gallop.

There was still a light in the front window as Lange pulled up. He heaved a sigh of relief when he saw there were no new horses tied at the rail. He fastened his own horse and headed for the front door. This time though, he knocked and waited for it to be opened to him.

'Charlie, what are you doing back so soon, pal? Come on in.'

Pete ushered him in to the warm kitchen. Rosie looked up, surprised to see him again so quickly and smiled broadly. She got up to pour him a coffee, but he refused it.

'Sorry, Rosie, but I got to head right back out. Just needed to know what Morten was telling you. You didn't let slip my real name, did you?'

He turned to Pete, a worried frown creasing his brow.

'No, of course we didn't. After I saw you that first day, I told Rosie something was wrong, and that if we saw you again, we all had to use the name of 'Lange'. That's what that feller said you were called when he came looking for you. Gave a good description of you, so I knew who he meant. I just went with it.'

'Good. Good, look, he's not as friendly as he seemed. He just wants to wangle out what he can about me. Anything at

186

all that he can use as ammunition against me. It's important I remain incognito to him, and to the others.'

'Others? What others? Hellfire, Charlie, what is it you've got yourself mixed up in? Is there anything we can do to help you?'

'All you can do is to remember that my name's Vince Lange, but here in town, right now, I'm going under the name of 'Fletcher'. I know it's damn confusing, but whatever you call me, for God's sake don't use my real name. Steer as clear as possible from Morten, and from any other strangers you might come across. If I tell you any more than that, all your lives will be in danger. I don't want that. Look, I've got to go; just wanted to check everything was OK here. I don't trust that goddamn bastard as far as I can spit. Sorry, Rosie.'

She smiled up at him, forgiving this lapse of manners easily in an old friend.

'Oh, Charlie. It's fine. But you do look awful. When Pete told me he'd seen you, I knew he was worried about you. Whatever it is you're up to, it's not doing you any good. You look so skinny and pale. Please, Charlie, do be careful.'

'Thanks Rosie. I'm fine, just a bit tired, is all. And I will be careful, don't you worry.'

He rested a hand gently on her shoulder and smiled down at her. She and Pete were the nearest he had to family, and he'd never be able to live with himself if anything happened to them. Rosie patted his hand, and he turned to leave.

He headed for the door, closely followed by Pete, who stood in the doorway watching as his friend mounted up again.

'You take care now, Charlie.'

Lange nodded and wheeled his horse. He rode back into town with his mind churning.

Everything was coming to a head. And it was all way too soon.

12

Lange didn't bother going over to the Rose again after he'd stabled his horse; simply went right to his room and threw himself down on the bed, trying to organize his jumbled thoughts.

This job was getting more and more complicated all the time, he was beginning to wish he hadn't volunteered. The only glimmer of hope was that the thaw meant they would soon be able to leave this town and get back out on the trail.

They were all going crazy, stuck in this place, pretending to be who they weren't for so long. It was only a matter of time before one of them cracked.

The thaw was progressing well now; the way would be free enough for a getaway almost any day. He was tense and irritable. He was having to try even harder to keep himself hidden from those townsfolk whom he had recognized up to now.

He'd managed pretty well for long enough. Pete was the only one who had actually challenged him so far, he reckoned he'd probably be fine for another week or two. Or until Carlin decided it was time for them to make the hit.

The Wells Fargo coach came into town every other Friday afternoon, to pick up the money from the bank and transport it to their head office. They'd been delayed for two visits now, because of the depth of the snow out on the flat lands, but Carlin had managed to discover that in the coming week they'd be back once more.

Their delay meant that there was a hell of a lot more cash in the safe than usual, which was fortuitous for the Carlin gang, but if they didn't hit the bank in the next week, before the Fargo coach turned up, then only a fraction of the cash would be there.

Carlin had told his men the hit would have to be at the last possible moment of the Thursday, just as the bank staff were closing everything up for the day.

Lange knew it would be up to him then, to try and stop the heist before it began, to minimize any damage or injury to the townsfolk. Carlin had decided it was up to Lange's alter ego, 'Fletcher', to act as the lookout, whilst the rest of the gang went into the bank and collected the cash and gold.

Lange was happy enough with that arrangement, in fact it couldn't have worked out any better. He could help the sheriff out from there. That was all supposing the sheriff had believed the notes that Pete had delivered. Lange had passed this latest information on to Pete again.

It wouldn't be long before the showdown. Then, Lange could go back to being the person he really was once more.

That moment couldn't come soon enough as far as he was concerned.

Thursday morning dawned bright, if still cold. The snow was melting fast now and the roads out of town were clear again. Once out on the trail, the Carlin gang would reach their hideout in just a couple of days. If they managed to get away with the heist, that was.

Lange was busying himself bagging up the feed, when he realized someone was watching him. Straightening up and rubbing at his back, he turned to see Carlin glaring at him.

'Howdy, boss.'

Carlin nodded, but he didn't speak, just kept staring at Lange with those cold snake eyes. Lange matched his stare.

'Something wrong?' Lange asked eventually.

'Nope. Just come to tell you there's been a change of plan, is all.'

'Oh yeah?'

Lange was uncomfortable; a change of plan so late would mean he couldn't get another message to the sheriff. That could pose a problem.

'Yeah. Morten's going to take look-out. You're coming into the bank with me and Skinner.'

Lange went cold. That meant the sheriff would believe Morten was actually

Lange, and would tell him what was going down. It also meant that Vince Lange would be pointing a gun at innocent people. He'd done that many times before, but this was different, these were people he knew.

Carlin thought nothing of killing in cold blood; if anyone in the bank put up a fight, they would most certainly die. Lange could only hope Pete had managed to convince the sheriff, and that his old friend would be around in order to clear up any unfortunate misunderstandings that might arise.

The worst of it was, had Lange been on lookout, he would have steered folk away from going into the bank all the while the gang were in there. Morten would simply encourage them to go in. Many more innocent people could be killed.

Damn! It was all going feet up. And there wasn't a thing Lange could do about it at this late stage. He could see that Carlin was judging his reactions, he knew he had to stay cool.

'Sure, OK, boss. It's a bit of a sudden

193

change, though. Something wrong?'

Carlin smiled slowly, his cold eyes glinting like steel in the shadows of the feed store, and the temperature dropped.

'Nope. Nothing wrong. Not now anyways. Everything's just dandy, kid. See you at the bank later, 'Fletcher," he snorted.

Carlin turned and left the building, leaving Lange feeling frustrated and angry. Damn the man! He must have got wind of something, somehow. That was why he'd changed the plan. Lange kicked at a sack of feed in his rage, then balled his fist and punched the wall.

It didn't help any.

People were still going to get hurt.

13

Lange got the chance to leave the feed store earlier than usual that day. He had to get to the bank before closing. Heading across town, he tightened his gun belt a notch. He knew what he had to do.

He could see the bank up ahead of him. Morten was leaning on the hitching rail outside; Lange slowed his pace some and watched as Carlin and Skinner wandered over from the Rose, both trying their best to look like innocent townsfolk and both failing miserably.

The two men didn't even acknowledge Morten, nor did they look to see if Lange was nearby. It had all been planned to the letter; they knew he'd be there. They entered the bank and he quickened his pace.

From the corner of his eye, he could see into the sheriff's office as he passed and noted, with a sense of satisfaction, both the sheriff and Pete were standing in there, apparently talking. Pete glanced up as his old friend passed, and their eyes met. Pete nodded.

As Lange approached the bank, Morten looked round at him and nodded. Lange needed to know who was in the bank besides Carlin and Skinner. He knew there were normally three tellers and the manager in there, and could only hope that none of the townsfolk had gone in, as he stood beside Morten at the hitching post.

'How's it going?' Lange whispered.

'Carlin wants you to go in soon as you get here. So get!'

As Lange headed for the door of the bank, he glanced around and spotted Pete and the sheriff, headed towards Morten, guns already drawn. With a crooked smile, Lange entered the bank. He heard the sounds of a scuffle just behind him as he went in.

Inside, Carlin was sitting at a desk; Skinner was pretending to read some paperwork on the bank wall. Carlin was talking to the bank manager and there were papers on the desk between them. Looking around, Lange could see no other customers, just the three tellers behind the screen, who were all busying themselves in cashing up the day's takings.

Lange drew closer to the manager's desk. Skinner looked up and nodded to him, then went back to his 'reading', but Lange noticed he loosened his iron in its holster as he did so.

'Yes, Mr Thomas, we just require a signature on these two forms and then you have your account. On behalf of the Pine Creek bank, I would like to welcome you.'

The bank manager reached out his hand across the desk to shake Carlin's.

All hell broke loose.

Carlin grabbed the manager's hand, heaving him over the desk, at the same time slicking his gun from the holster and levelling it right between the manager's eyes. Skinner pointed his own weapon at the tellers; Lange cleared leather to do the same. Carlin barked his orders, waving his Colt close to the manager.

'You. Go get the safe open. You lot behind there, put all the money you got into the bag. Fast! Fletcher, go lock the front door!'

Lange crossed to the door and slid the bolt, he could see shadows outside and knew they were waiting. Skinner threw a gunnysack over the screen to the tellers, who were sitting with their hands held high. Lange looked around for the young blonde woman he'd often seen in there, probably a secretary; she was nowhere to be seen. He only hoped she would realize what was going down and stay wherever she was.

Lange realized Pete must have been able to warn the sheriff in plenty of time, as there was no one else in the bank but the staff and Carlin's men. Four unarmed bank staff against three well-armed robbers. No one would think to take a chance against them, they wouldn't fancy their odds, not even if there was a gun under their counter.

'Jackson, Fletcher, cover 'em! You, show me the safe!'

Carlin motioned to the manager, who stood slowly from his desk and walked, hands raised, towards the door that led into the strong room where the safe was kept. It had to be now.

Lange took a shot at Skinner, hitting him in the gun arm. As Skinner dropped to the floor with a scream, grabbing at his shattered arm, Lange twisted and fired at Carlin, who had turned and raised his gun as soon as he heard the ruckus. Lange was much faster.

Carlin's Colt flew from his hand before he had the chance to fire a shot and he joined Skinner on the floor. The bank manager grabbed Carlin's gun and pointed it at him.

Lange picked up Skinner's weapon and was now levelling two weapons at the moaning man, who was clutching at his bleeding arm.

The tellers were ashen-faced, one was still holding on to the sack as he watched the scene unfurling before him. Lange still couldn't see the girl. She was obviously safe, though.

Carlin was cursing and spitting, as he held on to his arm and a pool of blood formed on the wooden floor beside him.

'You bastard! What in the hell are you playin' at? I'm gonna kill you, Lange! Slow as molasses in winter! You goddam, double-crossing bastard! You're gonna suffer for this! Listen here, mister?' Carlin looked up at the bank manager. 'That there feller, his name's Vince Lange, he's wanted everywhere, there's a good price on his head, you help me out of here and you get to keep it all!'

The manager shook his head slowly, keeping the gun directed at Carlin's head. Carlin was getting desperate.

'This other feller beside me, his name's Sam Skinner. He's just about as wanted as Lange. Help me, and keep 'em both. Whaddya say, mister?'

The manager just shook his head, silently. Lange pushed Skinner with the toe of his boot, and made him shuffle across the floor closer towards his boss. Skinner was spitting feathers.

'What the hell, Carlin! Sure, you try and save your own damn skin! Listen to me, mister! That there feller's name is John Carlin, he's wanted all over the damn country, and that guy holdin' the guns, he's Vince Lange just like Carlin said. I didn't do nothin'. I'm innocent! It's them you want! And what the hell's happened to Morten? He's supposed to be at the door. Where in the hell is he? He's just as wanted as them two. Me, I'm just an innocent bystander, I tell you. I didn't do nothin'!'

Lange looked at the manager and shook his head.

'You OK holding them both for just a second, sir, while I go and get the door open for the sheriff?'

'I most certainly am.'

Lange strolled to the door, smiling at the tellers as he went and saw them heave a collective sigh of relief as he passed them. He slid the bolt back from the door, letting the sheriff, Pete and a couple of deputies in. Pete hung back, standing close beside his friend as the sheriff and his men took over from the bank manager.

'What's happened to Morten?' Lange asked his friend.

'We sneaked up on him as you were coming in. Sheriff Black pistol-whipped the bastard, and we bundled him into the jail before he could call out. You OK?'

'Sure, takes more than these bastards to take me down, I reckon they were planning on taking me soon, though, judging from the way they've been behaving lately.'

He could hear Carlin protesting his innocence loudly now, and blaming the others for everything. The sheriff and his deputy had Carlin and Skinner in irons and were pushing them towards the door. Carlin stopped dead when he drew level with Lange. His icy stare burned into the younger man's innards.

'This feller! He's Vince Lange! He's at least as wanted as us! Arrest him!'

'Can't see any Vince Lange anywhere, mister. You must be mistaken.'

The sheriff looked at Lange, eyes twinkling. Carlin and Skinner struggled hard against their captors.

'Him! The tall one! He's Vince Lange! Take a look at your posters, you useless shit! He's a wanted man too!'

The sheriff looked from his prisoners to Lange and back again.

'Either of you two fellers actually *see* this man kill anyone?'

'Sure we did! He killed plenty!' Carlin yelled; Skinner nodded in agreement. The sheriff snorted, shaking his head slowly.

'That right? Hell, I doubt it. This here man's an undercover Deputy Marshall name of Charlie Dane. He got himself in with your gang 'cause you been so damn slippery over the years, kept disappearing. Nobody could figure out how you were doing it, so the Deputy Marshal here volunteered for special duty.' He turned to Lange and smiled. 'Thanks, Deputy, couldn't have done it without you. Come on over to the office when you have a minute, fill in the forms, OK?'

'Sure will, and then I'll take you to the

hideout. We can empty it and blast it, so it can't be used again. I'll see you in a while.'

With Carlin and Skinner spluttering and cursing between them about what they were going to do to Lange, the sheriff and his men hauled them off to join Morten in the jail.

The bank manager stepped forward and held out his hand to Dane.

'I have to thank you, Deputy Dane, you saved us today, saved the bank's money too. That was a good job, well done.'

Dane smiled and managed to drag his own hand back from the manager's, who was shaking it way too vigorously, with a huge smile on his pale face.

'That's OK, sir, all part of the job. By the way, I saw a young woman in here, behind the counter, a couple of times lately. Blonde hair, dainty. Is she OK?'

The manager smiled up at him.

'That would be my daughter, Martha. She *did* come in earlier today, but was feeling unwell, so, luckily I sent her off home. She's expecting my first grandchild, you see. She's married to young Ed over there. She's quite safe, in fact, I think we will make certain she stays at home for the remainder of her pregnancy, wouldn't want to risk this happening again, eh?'

Dane was relieved to hear that, for a while back there, he'd thought she was maybe going to come in while the heist was going down and create even more problems.

He and Pete left the bank and sauntered over to the sheriff's office. Pete clapped him on the shoulder and smiled broadly at him.

'So, 'Mr Lange' or 'Fletcher,' or Dane, which is it today? *This* was what you'd gotten yourself mixed up in. No wonder you were so secretive. I can see now why you warned us off that feller. D'you think, now they're behind bars, you'll get back to your normal job again?'

'Oh hell, yeah! I've had way more than my fill of secrets, Pete. Got real fed up of looking over my shoulder all the time in case anyone found anything out, having to be careful what I say, hiding out in caves. Yeah, I think I'll be taking it easy for a while now.'

'Caves? Hell, you can tell us *that* one later. Rosie asked if you'd like to come over for supper tonight?'

'Thanks. I'll be there, Pete, you can count on it. Your Rosie's a real good cook. Been a long time since I ate a good, home-cooked meal.'

As they entered the sheriff's office, they were hit full on by the sounds of the Carlin gang mouthing off about what they were going to do to 'Lange', and cursing him to Hell and back for double-crossing them all.

Sheriff Black closed the heavy wooden door leading to the cells, but that didn't stop the cussing, just deadened its volume a tad. He sat at his desk and pulled out a sheaf of paperwork, motioning to Dane to sit opposite.

'You'll be familiar with this stuff, eh? So I'll just give them to you to fill in and sign for me, I've already sent a telegraph for the judge to come over as soon as he's able. The sooner I can get rid of this lot the better I'll feel. You did a great job here, Mr Dane. Sorry, Deputy Marshal Dane. When will you be ready to take me out to the hideout?'

'How about we start tomorrow morning? It's getting dark now, we'd be better leaving it until daybreak, we need good light to climb that path.'

He was filling in the forms as he was talking.

'That's fine by me, Deputy Marshal Dane, I'll be ready by sunup.'

'Hey, name's Charlie. Forget the fancy handle. See you then. Be bringing Mr Mackie along, if that's OK by you?'

'Sure is, you're the boss here now, after all, whatever you say, Charlie.'

14

The following morning, the men met up outside the sheriff's office. They were taking along a buggy, both to fetch back the provisions that had been stashed there and to carry along the dynamite they were going to use to blow the cave.

One of the deputies, Jim, had been a miner and was used to handling the stuff, so with Jim driving the buggy, they headed off for the cave.

Dane wasn't overly keen on going back to the cave, but he reckoned this would be the end of it. Blasting the cave would mean no one else could use it as a hideout any longer at least, and that would permanently close this chapter of his life.

As they drew up at the base of the mountain, Sheriff Black looked around and whistled.

'The hideout's way up there somewhere? No wonder it was never found.

OK then, Charlie, you lead the way, Jim, you stay down here with the buggy and the mounts, I'll call out when we need you. Let's go.'

Charlie Dane began to lead the way up the familiar steep path, pausing at the entrance for Pete and Sheriff Black to catch him up.

As the other men reached the flat area outside the entrance, Dane signalled to them to hush up, he was studying the entrance door, something was wrong. The hair on his neck prickled.

Somehow, he could feel that there was someone in the cave; the door was in place, but it was wrong. He remembered how he'd left it, and this wasn't it. He quickly motioned the men behind to stop.

Best thing they could do now was to head back down to flat ground and re-think their plans. They could only hope that whoever was in the cave hadn't heard their approach. As quietly as they could, the men retraced their steps back down to the wagon, re-grouping while they decided how to tackle this latest problem.

After much discussion, it was decided that Charlie Dane would once more assume the persona of Vince Lange, head up to the cave alone, and try to parley with whoever was holed up there. Chances were it would be someone who would recognize his name from the dodgers and would welcome him into the shelter of the cave.

Once in the cave, Dane would over-power the guy, and when he was securely hog-tied in the wagon, they could do what they'd come for at last. It was risky, but if the plan didn't work, it could be weeks or more before they could flush the guy out.

No one had that sort of time to spare.

Dane began the walk up the steep path alone, Pete and Sheriff Black waiting be-hind the rocks at the base of the incline. As he went, Dane kept an ear open for any small sounds that might tell him the cave entrance was being opened.

Rounding Devil's Elbow with caution, Dane could see the cave opening prop-erly at last; it was still closed, so whoever was hiding in there hadn't heard their previous visit. He knew he needed to approach with care. Should he holler and let the inhabitant know he was there, or just ease open the door and try sneaking in, ambushing whoever was on the other side?

He paused for a moment while he let his brain toss over the problem. There was no way of telling who might be inside. One person he could manage, a whole gang would be a problem.

Mind made up, he slowly opened the door and as he squeezed in, he whistled loudly, and called out.

'Hello, the cave!'

Immediately there was the sound of someone scurrying around, and Dane heard the loud report of a gun being cocked, before a voice called back to him.

'Who the hell are you, mister? And what you doin' up here?'

'I'm coming up and we can talk.'

'You can stay right there, mister. Whaddya want, how'd you find this place?'

'Name's Vince Lange, I'm one of Carlin's men. We live here. So by rights, I should be asking how you got here, and who the hell you are.'

'Lange? The Preacher? I heard about you. Come on up, easy like, let me look at you.'

Dane eased his way up the tunnel to the cave, and as he rounded the last corner, he was greeted by a rifle thrust in his face. He raised his hands, and took stock. A rangy horse and a scruffy-looking mule were tied up in the corner.

The man was dirty and unkempt, with long matted hair and a beard that looked as if it was full of the remains of his last few meals, but his hands on the rifle were steady as he stared at the newcomer.

Dane stood quietly, hands in the air, whilst the man looked him up and down. Dane could see that the contents of the niches all still seemed to be intact; there was an untidy bedroll in the middle of the floor, and a couple of torches were burning in their improvised sconces, but he couldn't see a fire.

'Can you spare a cup, mister?' he asked eventually.

'Ain't got no fire. If'n I lit one in here, I'd be smoked out in no time. Huh! I don't reckon you lived up here, or you'd know that little fact, mister. Who the hell are you?'

'I told you, name's Vince Lange, I've been riding with Carlin around two years now. This here's our hideout. You must have seen the dodgers for us, don't you recognize me?'

'OK, hands down, put your gun away, let's parley. If you and Carlin used this here place, how come you didn't smoke yourselves out then?'

He sat on one of the large rocks, still holding the primed rifle. Dane holstered his gun and sat on another large stone, quick eyes taking in all he could about the man.

'What's your name, mister?'

'Who's holding the gun, kid? I heard about the 'Preacher man' on the rounds. Tales are you'se a blood-thirsty bastard. That right?' He frowned down the barrel.

213

'I guess.'

'So tell me how to get a fire goin' in here? I'm starved. Ran off from a posse in Lawton, couple weeks back, I'd heard 'bout this place from Carlin once, so when I found myself hereabouts, I reckoned I'd come lookin' for him and see 'bout joining him. Only there ain't nobody here. Where's he at?'

'There was a shoot-out in Viper Creek, I got away, I think Carlin was caught, I guess I'm the only one who's made it back here up to now. Hopefully some of the others'll turn up soon.'

'Yeah. It'd be a shame if Carlin was dead, he was a good man.'

Good wasn't exactly the word Charlie Dane would have used when mentioning Carlin, but he went along with the other man.

'Yeah, well, maybe he'll turn up, he could always talk himself out of sticky situations. You say you got no fire, want me to show you where we build it?'

'Can't see any trace round here, Preacher man, you sure you had fires?'

'Sure, we couldn't have stayed hidden up here as long as we did without them. Let me show you, then we can get a pot of coffee on the go, and get warmed up some, eh?'

The man nodded and lowered his rifle, releasing the trigger, but still watching Dane closely, he nodded. Dane got up and walked slowly past him.

'What did you say you were called, mister?' he asked casually as he passed the man.

'I didn't. It's Roberts, John Roberts, and I reckon there's almost as many wanted posters out for me as there are for you, Preacher.'

Dane nodded, he recognized the name. Roberts' details were well-known to him. There was a price on the man's head, not a great one, but hell, every little helps.

'OK, follow me, Mr Roberts, the fire bed's out this away.'

He began to lead the man up the dog-leg towards the rear entrance. As they reached the right-angle at the end, Dane suddenly turned and smashed his fist into the other man's face, felling him instantly. The rifle dropped to the floor. Lange picked it up and levelled it at Roberts, where he lay, rubbing at his face and wondering what the hell had just happened to him.

'OK, Mr Roberts. Up you get, we're off to visit the sheriff.'

'Damn you! I heard you was a cunning bastard. Shoulda kept the gun on you, I guess. Come on, we're both on the run, take me into town and you'll be in trouble too. I won't keep my mouth shut about who you are.'

'Nope, I guess you won't. Come on, scoot on back to the cave, hands behind you.'

'Fer Pete's sake! We could work together. I heard Carlin had a stash of gold hidden away up here someplace, you must know where it is. What say we split it and go our own ways?'

'Sorry. I don't reckon so. That money belongs to the people it was stolen from.'

'Hah! You're soundin' like a damn lawman now, Preacher. C'mon, kid, there's gotta be enough for both of us.'

They reached the cave, Dane grabbed up a rope and fastened Robert's hands securely behind his back.

'Yep, there would be enough for both of us, and more, but just for now, it stays right where it is. Go on, head on out.'

'What about the animals?'

'I'll be back for them. Head out.' He nudged the man in the back with the rifle. Roberts staggered down the tunnel in front of Dane.

As the two men appeared at the cave entrance, Dane called out to let the other men know he was coming out. Roberts turned to him, a look of pure hatred on his dirty face.

'Damn it! You are a lawman! How'd you get in with Carlin? If he'd known what you were …'

'Shut it and keep walking.'

The rifle nudged him again, none too gently, and he began to stumble his way down the rocky path. Dane could see Pete and the sheriff waiting for them, guns at the ready.

'You sneaky little — '

'Yeah, yeah, yeah! I heard you, now move. You're going to join your friend Carlin in the lock up to wait for the county judge; we'll see what *he* wants to do with you in due course.'

The rest of their way down was accompanied by Roberts swearing and cursing, and loud threats as to what he was going to do to 'Lange' when he got free.

As they got to the flat land at last, Sheriff Black stepped forward and shoved a bandanna in Robert's mouth and locked a pair of handcuffs to his wrists.

'Now, will you shut up? Hell, we could hear your yakkin' from down here! It's given me a headache! Come on, I'll fasten you in the wagon while we finish up here.'

Roberts was secured hand and foot in the wagon, and Dane, Pete and Sheriff Black headed back for the cave, leaving Roberts in the care of Jim, the deputy.

Between them, the three men removed the entrance door and entered the tunnel, leading their horses. Dane took a torch from its hole on the wall just inside the entrance and lit it; the shadows cast by the bright flames outlined the lumps and crevices on the walls of the low entrance way. Pete whistled.

'So this is where you were living. If I'd known you were here, I'd have called in!'

The three men laughed as they carried on along the tunnel and finally entered the large cave. As Sheriff Black and Pete wandered around, looking closer at the items stashed in there, Charlie Dane went across to his own corner and began to organize his belongings. The sheriff whistled low as he reached up and pulled the boxes of ammunition from their niche.

'You fellers sure made this place homely. Coulda held off an army with this lot, I reckon.'

Pete was collecting the dry goods together and stacking them close to the entrance. When Dane had finished in his corner, he helped Pete and the sheriff to load up the horses and Roberts's mule. They reckoned they'd have to make a few trips up and down to load up the wagon, there were so many boxes and bags to move.

Eventually, the cave was empty of all signs of human habitation, and Jim fetched the blasting caps and powder up from the buggy. He looked around the cave to find the best places to lay the charges. But before they were ready, Dane called the sheriff over to the place where the strongbox was buried.

'Reckoned we'd best leave this 'till last. No sense in leaving it out there in the open while we're all in here, especially with Roberts watching, and you never know who might be riding by, eh?'

Dane knelt down and began pulling away the stones and digging into the sand. With some effort, he pulled the strongbox out into the centre of the cave, and looked up at the sheriff.

'You did bring Carlin's key with you?'

'Sure did.'

He passed it to Dane, who opened the lid on to a fortune in money, jewellery and gold. The men crowded together to look at the contents of the strongbox. Sheriff Black spoke first.

'Hellfire! There's a lot of money in that there box. How long d'you reckon it took to get that much?' he asked Dane.

'Well, I've been with Carlin nigh on two years, it was being used when I first came here, so couple or three years, maybe more. That's stuff from banks, hotels, telegraph offices, hell, everywhere. A lot of the jewels were taken from women in the stages we held up, some from those unlucky enough to be in the banks we hit. Maybe you can find some of the owners?'

'I'll have a damn good try. I guess Fargo better get involved, they have ways of finding folk, and anyway, some of this would be theirs by rights, eh?'

'We never hit a Fargo coach, but there's a fair bit from banks and other such places, so I guess by that reckoning, yes, it would.'

Dane and Pete carried the strongbox down to the waiting buggy, while the sheriff and his deputy laid the charges, and followed them down to the flat lands at the foot of the mountains. Jim unrolled the fuse as far away from the rocks as was possible, the buggy and horses were taken a safe distance away and Sheriff Black gave Jim the order.

In moments, a huge explosion thundered through the air, the ground trembled, the horses shied and pranced as a storm of sand and shale rained down from the cloud surrounding the top of the mountain.

The men sat quietly and watched, as the tip of the mountain slowly shrunk, and disintegrated before their eyes. The men and animals were covered with a layer of dust and small pebbles even at the distance they were from it.

As soon as they were sure the cave was gone, the group headed back for the town, with Roberts struggling and kicking in the back of the buggy, surrounded by the boxes and sacks of foodstuffs and ammunition.

15

Once they reached the town, Sheriff Black headed for the telegraph office whilst his deputy, Dane and Pete unloaded the wagon. Roberts was placed in a cell, and he and the remaining Carlin gang members got to cursing each other straightaway.

Dane, Jim and Pete took everything from the wagon and put them into one of the empty cells, piling them up as tidily as they could, all the time being assailed by Carlin's curses.

Pete went off home to his family, with a solemn promise from his old friend Charlie Dane that he would come by for his tea that night. The three lawmen set to, sorting the haul and trying to match it up with the list of stolen goods the sheriff held.

Dane had to tell Sheriff Black about the Levin family. Turned out they hadn't been into the town at all, so he wasn't able to tell Dane anything about them, but took the details to keep on record should anyone come looking for them.

All the time, their work was accompanied by Carlin and his men cussing and threatening both them and Roberts, and Roberts cussing and threatening them in turn.

'I'll be glad when the circuit judge gets here. Not sure how long I can put up with all that there racket,' said the sheriff, smiling as they counted out the stolen notes on his desk.

'The damn lot of 'em are enough to give the Devil a headache, never heard so much racket,' Jim agreed.

'Well, I'm going to leave you fellers to their gentle songs, I got a real good meal waiting for me over at Pete's place.'

Dane signed off the papers the sheriff handed him, touched his hat in salute and left the office with a spring in his step. He felt lighter than he had in a good while as he mounted up and headed towards Pete's place.

The following day, Charlie Dane had decided he'd leave the town and head off on a journey of his own. As he packed up his saddle-bags once more, tucking his silver star back into its secret hiding place, he sighed deeply. He was growing tired of this undercover work.

Sure, it paid well, but after spending last night with Pete and Rosie and their little ones, he'd started to think it was maybe time he got himself a job where he could stay in one place.

He'd settle down; maybe get himself a wife and kids. Possibly even settle round this place, he had some good friends here after all. First, though, he had a mission.

He took the locket from its pouch, and opened it. Miss Levin's pale face challenged him. It challenged him to find her, to give her back her rightful property, and tell her what had happened to her folks. He sighed again, how could he tell her what had happened? How could he explain his part in that? If he ever did find her, he'd lie to her, he knew he would. If he ever found her.

Later, mounting up, he looked around the town one more time. Yep, this was just the sort of place he'd like to finally settle down in. Maybe even get himself a peaceable sort of job. Maybe, one day.

As he passed the sheriff's office, the sheriff was sitting outside, they nodded to one another, and as Dane passed he could hear, even from outside, the harsh sound of Carlin's voice, hurling his loud and colourful profanities at everyone.

He and his gang would soon be pushing up the daisies, and that thought gave Charlie Dane a feeling of such satisfaction that he smiled broadly, as he urged his mount into a loping trot away from the town.

Maybe he'd just stick at this job a little while longer after all.